THE HOLIDAY SPIRIT

Veronica turned to Stevie. "You haven't been doing anything to my locker, have you?" she asked, her green eyes narrowing.

"No," Stevie replied with a clear conscience. "I've been talking to Carole and Lisa."

Veronica slowly began to open the door an inch at a time, as if she expected a rubber snake to come bursting out. Finally Veronica opened the door all the way. Everything in the locker seemed normal.

Stevie, Carole, and Lisa tried hard not to laugh as Veronica then turned each boot upside down and shook it before she pulled it onto her foot. Next she checked the pockets of her jacket to make sure nothing disgusting had been hidden there.

"Well," she said airily, trying to disguise the nervousness in her voice. "Everything seems fine. See you in class."

"Have a good lesson," Stevie called. "And don't forget to check your stirrup leathers. You never know what can happen around here at Christmastime!"

Other books you will enjoy

CAMY BAKER'S HOW TO BE POPULAR IN THE SIXTH GRADE
by Camy Baker

CAMY BAKER'S LOVE YOU LIKE A SISTER *by Camy Baker*

ANNE OF GREEN GABLES *by L. M. Montgomery*

HORSE CRAZY (The Saddle Club #1) *by Bonnie Bryant*

AMY, NUMBER SEVEN (Replica #1) *by Marilyn Kaye*

PURSUING AMY (Replica #2) *by Marilyn Kaye*

FOUL PLAY (Soccer Stars #1) *by Emily Costello*

THE SADDLE CLUB
SUPER EDITION #7

CHRISTMAS TREASURE

BONNIE BRYANT

A SKYLARK BOOK
NEW YORK · TORONTO · LONDON · SYDNEY · AUCKLAND

RL 5, 009–012

CHRISTMAS TREASURE

A Bantam Skylark Book / December 1998

*I would like to express my special thanks
to Sallie Bissell for her
help in the writing of this book.*

"STEVIE, THIS IS one of the craziest things you've ever done!" Carole Hanson shivered in the cold morning air as she tiptoed behind her friend Stevie Lake. "I feel like I'm in some kind of spy movie!"

"Shhh!" Stevie edged along the back wall of Pine Hollow Stables. "Don't talk so loud. Max might hear us." Stevie spoke in a whisper, her breath coming out in frosty puffs of smoke.

"I don't understand why we can't just walk in through the stable like everybody else," Carole complained as she sneaked through the frozen grass. "So you're late to Horse Wise. Everybody is late to something sometime in their life."

"But I was late for the last Horse Wise meeting and my riding lesson on Wednesday. This makes the third time in two weeks. And you know how Max is about that!" Max Regnery, the owner of Pine Hollow, was an excellent horseman and wonderful teacher, but he didn't approve of people being late. Stevie had seen his blue eyes flash with disapproval more than once.

"If we can sneak into Horse Wise without him seeing us, he'll never know we're late."

Carole frowned as she crept along behind her best friend. "But he's probably conducting the Horse Wise meeting now. He won't notice we're late if he's busy talking."

"I can't take the chance," Stevie replied. She stopped suddenly under a window, rose on tiptoe, and peeked in. "It's just as I thought," she reported in a hoarse whisper. "They're meeting in the indoor riding ring. It looks like they're watching some slides. We'll have to sneak through the door in the back. Otherwise, Max will see us."

"Is Lisa there?" Carole craned her neck and tried to peek over Stevie's shoulder.

"I can't see her, but I'm sure she is," Stevie said. "Lisa's never late for anything." Lisa Atwood was Stevie and Carole's other best friend and the third member of the Saddle Club, a club the girls had started sometime earlier. The club had only two rules—that the members had to be crazy about horses, and that they had to help each other out at all times. Of the three girls, Lisa was the oldest and most responsible. Carole was the craziest about horses, and Stevie was mostly just the craziest. Stevie was almost as good at getting into trouble as Carole and Lisa were at getting her out of it.

The two girls crunched through the stiff grass to the back door and peeked inside. The indoor ring was dark, and all the members of the Horse Wise Pony Club were seated in front of a portable movie screen, on which Max was showing slides of horses jumping. This was the last Horse Wise meeting before the Christmas holidays, and the girls knew that Max would announce Pine Hollow's party plans. They both hoped they hadn't missed that part already.

Stevie inched into the darkened arena and motioned for Carole to follow her around the shadowy edges of the ring.

The slide projector clicked. A picture of a gray horse leaping over a double oxer flashed up on the screen. "This horse is going to land properly," Max's voice said, echoing in the dimness. "His legs are well out in the front, and he's got a lot of impulsion from behind. The rider's hands are also in good position, and he's looking straight ahead with soft eyes."

Everyone studied the slide; then Max cleared his throat. "There are two other riders I know of right now who aren't showing such good form," he said. "They're way out of position, their seats are definitely in the wrong place, and instead of having soft eyes, they've got a wild and terrified look in them. Welcome, Stevie and Carole. Glad you could join us." Max's gaze never left the screen.

Everyone turned and looked toward the back door. A chorus of laughter erupted as everybody discovered Carole and Stevie in the dark edges of the arena. With sheepish grins, the two girls stopped creeping like cat burglars and hurried over to the rest of the riders.

"Sorry, Max," said Stevie as they picked their way through the crowd to sit beside Lisa. "Carole would have been on time, except I overslept and made us both late."

"Just take your seats quickly. If you're very lucky, I may overlook this, since it's so close to Christmas," Max said. "Please try to stay awake for the rest of these slides."

Everyone laughed again, and the meeting continued. Max showed slides of horses jumping both properly and improperly, mostly because of the aids given by their riders. After Max had described how good riders could help their horses be better jumpers, the slide show ended and he turned on the lights.

"Any questions?" he asked.

Two riders had questions about jumping. Then Veronica diAngelo, the snootiest, richest girl at Pine Hollow Stables, raised her hand.

Max nodded at her. "Yes, Veronica?"

"Are we going to have a Christmas party this year?"

Max frowned. He seemed tired lately, and the little lines around his eyes had grown deeper. "Well, Veronica, that's not exactly a question about jumping, but I suppose I'm glad you brought it up. Yes, we are having a party. It's going to be the night before Christmas Eve, and it's going to be in here, in the indoor ring." Max looked at the riders and gave a sly grin. "There's one thing, though, that we're going to be doing a little differently this year."

"What?" asked one of Veronica's friends, Betsy Cavanaugh.

"In years past at Pine Hollow we've always drawn names and given each other gifts. This year we're not going to be giving anything in the usual sense. This year we're going to be a different kind of Secret Santa."

Stevie's hand waved in the air. "Different?"

Max nodded. "That's right, Stevie. Instead of giving gifts, we'll each draw a name and do something for that person."

"Do something *for* that person or something *to* that person?" asked Joe Novick with a laugh.

"*For* that person, Joe," replied Max. "Remember, it's the holiday season, and we should all be doing good deeds. But it's up to you to figure out what thing your person needs to have done—something they wouldn't ordinarily do for themselves. You've got a little less than two weeks to get your good deed accomplished; then we'll reveal the Secret Santas at the Christmas party." Max looked around the group. "Any questions?"

A buzz of excitement rippled through the Horse Wise riders. Stevie and Carole and Lisa looked at each other. No gifts this year, only good deeds. This Christmas was going to be really different!

"Okay, then." Max pulled a riding helmet from the shelf under the slide projector. "This helmet has slips of paper with everybody's name in it. I'm going to bring it around and let everyone draw one slip. You'll be the Secret Santa to the person whose name is on that paper. Remember, don't show your slip to anyone, or tell whose name you drew!"

Max held the helmet at waist level and began to weave through the seated riders. Everyone closed their eyes, reached into the helmet, and withdrew a slip of paper. Some people laughed when they read the name they'd drawn; others wore looks of total disbelief. Slowly Max worked his way around the edges of the group. At last he came over to the Saddle Club.

"Okay, girls," he said. "Remember, this is a secret!" He shook the helmet, then held it out to Lisa. She reached up, drew a slip of paper, and read it quickly. A smile played across her lips; a second later her blue eyes clouded with puzzlement.

Max held the helmet out to Carole. She fumbled among the papers for a moment, then withdrew a slip. She read it and quickly stuffed it into the pocket of her breeches. Though she was smiling, her brows came together in a thoughtful frown as she stared at the toe of Lisa's boot.

Max moved on to Stevie, holding the helmet above her head. "Now, Stevie, you've got to get this done by December twenty-third. Under no circumstances can you be late with your Secret Santa job!"

"I know, Max." Stevie looked up at him, her hazel eyes serious. "I won't be. I promise." She reached up and grabbed the first slip of paper her fingers touched. Quickly she unfolded it and read the name. Before she could stop herself, she gave a little gasp, and her mouth curved downward in a horrified grimace. Of all the names she could have drawn from the helmet, this one was the worst possible name in the world!

"Okay." Max hurried back to the projector stand. "The helmet's empty. Did everybody draw a name, and are there any more questions about the Christmas party or the Secret Santas?"

No one raised a hand. "Then Horse Wise is adjourned," Max said with a smile. "If you guys do any jumping this week, try to remember to give your horses the proper aids. I'll see all of you back here at the Christmas party, and don't forget to keep your Secret Santas secret!"

"Whew," breathed Stevie as the girls stood up. "That was a close one! I thought Max would be furious at me."

"I think he might be too busy to be furious," Carole said, watching as Max dashed out of the indoor ring.

"How come you guys were late?" asked Lisa. "Carole, I thought you and your dad were giving Stevie a ride."

"We did," Carole answered. "Stevie just overslept."

Stevie grinned, remembering how she'd tumbled into the Hansons' car, pulling on her jacket and eating a piece of toast at the same time. "We had a really long play practice at school yesterday. Auditions are coming up next week, and my teacher wants us all to be prepared, so he's helping people practice their monologues, songs, whatever." She yawned and ran her hands through her tousled dark blond hair. "I guess I was more tired than I thought."

"Looks like you're still half-asleep." Lisa laughed, then remembered the crumpled slip of paper in her hand. "How did you guys like who you drew for Secret Santa?"

"Mine's going to be very difficult," said Carole with a note of mystery in her voice.

"Mine is, too." Lisa carefully folded the paper and stashed it in her pocket. "I don't have a clue about what my good deed's going to be."

"Really?" said Stevie, rolling her slip of paper into a tiny ball. "Mine's not difficult at all. Mine is horrible." She shuddered. "I don't even want to think about it."

"Then let's go on a trail ride," suggested Carole. "That way we can forget about being Secret Santa to anybody but our horses for a while."

"Sounds good to me," Lisa said. "Let's meet at the horseshoe. Last one tacked up's a rotten egg!"

The girls scurried off to their horses' stalls. Carole found her bay gelding, Starlight, happily munching hay, while Stevie's mare, Belle, was nosing around her stall for any spilled oats that might be hidden in the straw. Prancer, the ex-racehorse Lisa rode, was curled up like a deer, dozing in the winter sunlight.

"Wake up, lazybones," Lisa said, laughing. "You're as bad as Stevie!"

Prancer scrambled to her feet. In just a few minutes the mare was tacked up. Lisa buckled on her riding helmet and led Prancer outside.

It was a tradition at Pine Hollow to touch the horse-shoe that was nailed up by the entrance before every ride. So far everyone had honored that tradition, and no one had ever been seriously injured. By the time Lisa got there both Stevie and Carole were mounted up and ready to go.

"Somebody I know's a rotten egg," Carole sang softly.

"I know," Lisa said, pressing one finger against the horseshoe. "Prancer was still dozing when I got to her stall. We're ready now, though. Which trail shall we take?"

"Let's do the field trail," Stevie said as Belle shook her thick mane. "We did the mountain trail last week."

"Okay." Lisa climbed up on Prancer. "We can use the practice."

The three girls rode their horses up the hill behind the stable. Though the air was cold and crisp, the December sunshine sparkled, and the frost that still covered the delicate limbs of the trees glittered, giving everything a festive close-to-Christmas feel. Even the horses seemed to sense the excitement in the air. They all trotted up the hill briskly as if they, too, were looking forward to a holiday.

"I feel the need for speed," said Stevie, her nose already rosy from the cold. "We can go all the way to the end of the field and come back by the creek."

"Good idea." Carole patted Starlight's neck. "These guys are really frisky today. A nice long run will calm them down."

"Okay," said Lisa with a laugh. "Let's go!"

Stevie urged Belle into a fast canter. Carole and Lisa followed. They galloped through a small stand of trees, then across the broad yellow fields that opened before them. When the trail wound down into the woods next to the river, Stevie slowed Belle to a walk.

"Wasn't that wonderful?" she said, almost out of breath. "I think having sunny weather in December is terrific. It makes you feel so energetic!"

"It is nice," admitted Carole as she and Lisa pulled up beside Stevie. "But I really wish we'd have a big snow. Snow makes Christmas and Kwanzaa so much more special."

"I know what you mean." Lisa smiled. "Snow just seems to make everything all the more beautiful."

"Horses like snow, too," said Stevie. "Or at least Belle

does. She and I had a wonderful bareback ride when it snowed last winter."

The girls rode down the trail to the river, enjoying the combination of warm sun and frosty air. They watched as a pair of cardinals ate bright red berries from a holly bush. A fat gray squirrel scurried under an oak tree, digging up the acorns he'd buried in the fall.

"Seeing all these animals munching nuts and berries is making me hungry," said Stevie, clutching her stomach. "Why don't we ride back and then have some ice cream at TD's?"

Carole shook her head. "Stevie, it's about twenty degrees out here. How could you possibly think about eating ice cream?"

"Well, the sun's out." Stevie glanced at the sky. "That makes it ice cream weather to me!"

Lisa shivered inside her warm jacket. "Actually, food doesn't sound too bad. Maybe hot chocolate, though, instead of a chocolate malt."

"Okay, then, let's go. On to TD's!" Stevie turned Belle around.

"Let's take the shortcut through the field and jump the creek," Carole said. "That way we'll get to the stables faster."

"Okay," agreed Stevie. "You and Starlight lead the way."

Carole and Starlight took off in an easy canter, with

Stevie and Lisa following. The golden fields flew by as the horses raced back toward the stable. Soon Starlight and Carole were approaching the creek. As the big bay gelding neared the bank, Carole remembered the slides Max had shown at Horse Wise. She shifted her weight forward in the saddle as she felt Starlight begin to collect his hind legs under him, and she loosened her hold on the reins as he leaped into the air. For an instant they were flying; then, just as fast, they were landing smoothly on the other bank. Carole smiled and gave Starlight a pat. Every time she jumped a horse she remembered why it was one of her favorite things in the world to do.

Stevie and Belle were approaching the creek at the same easy canter, and at the same spot as Starlight, Belle collected herself and vaulted over the creek. Stevie came down softly in the saddle, then pulled up beside Carole to watch Lisa.

"Hurry up!" Stevie called as Lisa and Prancer neared the creek. "You're still the rotten egg!"

"We're coming," Lisa called. She urged Prancer on a little faster and shifted her weight forward in the saddle. The pretty bay mare picked up speed, but when she reached the spot where Belle and Starlight had begun their jump, she abruptly stiffened her legs and came sliding to a halt.

"Ouch!" cried Lisa, scooting forward in the saddle and bumping her nose on Prancer's neck.

13

"Are you okay?" called Stevie.

"Yes." Lisa rubbed her nose. "Just shocked. Prancer hasn't shied at water in months!"

"Turn her around and try it again," advised Carole. "Maybe the creek just took her by surprise."

"Good idea." Lisa turned Prancer around, then reapproached the creek at a brisk trot. Again, at the very same spot where Belle and Starlight had leaped into the air, Prancer stopped and planted herself firmly on the ground.

"She still won't do it," said Lisa, shaking her head. "But at least I didn't bump my nose this time."

"Try and walk her over it," Carole suggested. "Maybe she's just having a bad creek day."

Lisa urged Prancer forward at a walk. The mare took a few steps toward the water, then slapped her ears back and refused to move at all.

"This is terrible!" cried Lisa. "Her water problems have all come back, and I worked so hard to get her over them. I was even planning to ride her in the Fairfax Competitive Trail Ride next month. We can't enter if she stops dead still at every mud puddle!"

Stevie and Carole looked at each other and frowned. "Maybe you should just get off and lead her across," said Stevie. "I've got a carrot you can reward her with when she gets over here."

"Okay." Lisa sighed. She dismounted and pulled the reins over Prancer's head. "Come on, girl," she whispered, beginning to walk toward the creek. At first Prancer didn't budge, but Lisa gave a firm tug on her reins and she began to inch toward the water. "Come on, Prancer, it's okay," Lisa said gently, stepping into the shallow water. Prancer sniffed the water dubiously, then suddenly bolted across the creek. Lisa held the reins and ran along after her as she scrambled up the little bank.

"Whew," Lisa said, taking the carrot Stevie held out. "That's hardly what I'd call a smooth crossing."

"Maybe she just didn't want to get her feet wet," said Stevie, giggling. "That water must feel like ice."

Lisa watched Prancer chomp her carrot. "Yes, but if she'd jumped to begin with, her feet wouldn't be wet at all."

"Oh, don't worry about it," said Carole. "She's probably just been ridden too much by Max's novice students. She'll calm down once you start training for the competition."

"I hope so," said Lisa as she climbed into the saddle.

They rode slowly back to Pine Hollow, allowing the horses to cool down on the way. Prancer was again her usual cooperative self. She responded to all Lisa's aids, and by the time they reached the stable, the girls had only to untack the horses and give them a quick rubdown.

"I hope I'll have time to cure you of your water phobia before the competition next month," Lisa told Prancer as she toweled the mare's legs. When Prancer's legs and hooves were dry, Lisa gave her a lump of sugar and walked over to meet Stevie and Carole at Belle's stall.

"Bye, Belle," Stevie was saying, watching as Belle munched the bright red apple Stevie had brought for her. "We're off to get our own treats at TD's. Let's see. I wonder what I'll have today . . . maybe a chocolate and pistachio sundae with bubble gum bits. Or maybe a pineapple and pretzel surprise."

"Come on, Stevie," said Carole. "If you don't cool it with your bizarre ice cream treats you're going to make the horses sick!"

The girls walked toward TD's, the ice cream shop that was the site of most of their official and unofficial Saddle Club meetings. The other shops in the small shopping center were busy; customers bustled about with packages in their arms. Christmas music was being piped into the parking lot from the supermarket, and huge green wreaths with bright red bows hung from every lamppost.

"Wow," said Lisa as they walked past the brightly decorated shop windows. "It looks like Christmas is in full swing here."

They opened the door of TD's. Although red and green Christmas lights had been draped from the ceiling and the radio was playing Christmas music, the place was empty. The girls hurried to their favorite corner booth and took off their coats.

"It sure feels good and toasty in here today," said Carole as she untied the wool scarf around her neck.

"Most anyplace south of the North Pole would feel warm today," said Stevie, sliding into the booth.

16

The waitress who always served them made her way to their table. Usually she wore a plain white uniform. Today, though, she'd added a red sweater with a sprig of holly pinned to it. "What'll it be today, ladies?" she asked pleasantly.

"I'll have hot chocolate, please," said Lisa.

"Me too," said Carole.

"A wise choice," the waitress remarked as she scribbled on her pad. She gave Stevie a wary look. "And for you?"

"Uh, I'll have one scoop of pistachio ice cream with strawberry sauce and coconut sprinkles," Stevie said with a smile. "In honor of Christmas."

"Christmas?" The waitress raised one eyebrow.

Stevie nodded. "The pistachio's green, the strawberry sauce is red, the coconut's white. Christmas colors."

"I see." The waitress shook her head in disbelief. "Coming right up."

Lisa giggled as the waitress walked back to the counter. "Only you, Stevie, would order ice cream in Christmas colors!"

"Well, you've got to get into the spirit of the season."

"Speaking of the spirit of the season . . . ," Carole began.

"Oh, please, let's not discuss our Secret Santas," begged Stevie. "Mine is just too grim to talk about."

Carole smiled. "No, I wasn't going to talk about Secret Santas. I wanted to ask you guys if you'd like to help me and my dad out."

17

"Sure," said Lisa. "Doing what?"

"Well, he and a lot of other Marines have worked really hard all year on their annual toy drive. You know, that's where the Marines collect money and toys for needy children at Christmas. It's a great thing to do for little kids who won't have much of a Christmas otherwise."

"And?" Stevie smiled politely as the waitress returned with two cups of steaming hot chocolate and a dish of pale green ice cream covered in red sauce and little white curls of coconut.

"And now, since it's getting close to the holidays, a lot of Marines will be on leave. My dad's in charge of the whole operation this year, and he's going to need some extra help distributing the toys."

"That sounds like fun," said Lisa, stirring melted marshmallows into her hot chocolate. "I'd be glad to help. Only first I've got to help my mother cook about a million different Scottish dishes and clean our house. Our cousins are coming over from Scotland to spend Christmas with us."

"Really?" Stevie took a big bite of her ice cream. "I didn't know you had any relatives in Scotland."

Lisa nodded. "The Rosses. Sarah Ross is my mom's first cousin. She'll be coming with her husband, James, and their children, Eliot, Douglas, and twin toddlers."

"Wow," said Carole. "That's a lot of people."

"Tell me about it." Lisa rolled her eyes. "I don't know

where we're all going to sleep, much less eat and celebrate Christmas." She took a sip of her hot chocolate. "But I'll be glad to help you and your dad whenever I can."

"Me too," said Stevie. "But I'll have to help between rehearsals for the Christmas play. After all, I'm going to be singing the solo."

"Oh, Stevie! I didn't know you'd gotten the solo." Carole's dark eyes grew wide. "That's fantastic!"

"Well, I haven't exactly, officially gotten it yet. But I know I will. I mean, I've taken weekly voice lessons from Ms. Bennefield since October, and I've bought a new dress and I've even invited Phil to come and see me." Stevie licked strawberry sauce off the back of her spoon. "Anyway, my only competition for the part is Veronica diAngelo, who's managed to be an even bigger jerk at rehearsals than she is at the stable."

"I didn't think that was possible," said Lisa.

"It is, though," Stevie replied. "You wouldn't believe how she runs around the stage bossing everybody like she's some big star. I mean, we're only rehearsing the chorus parts right now, so everyone is supposed to be equal. But not Veronica! The lights have to be perfect, everybody has to know their lines exactly, and heaven help anybody who has to cough or sneeze when she's 'getting in touch with her character.' She is one royal pain. I don't know what I'll do if she gets the solo."

"I didn't even know Veronica could sing, much less

19

act." Carole warmed her hands around her cup of hot chocolate.

"She can't," said Stevie. "Every time she opens her mouth she sounds like a cat that's caught its tail in a lawn mower."

Carole and Lisa both burst into giggles. "Stevie, that's awful!"

"I know." Stevie shrugged. "But it's true."

"When is your play going to be?" Lisa asked.

"The same day as the Pine Hollow Christmas party," Stevie answered. "But don't worry. I'll have time to sing and chat with my adoring fans and still come to the Christmas party."

"We'll be sure and tell everybody at the stable to bring their autograph books." Carole laughed.

"Yes," said Lisa. "I know they'd hate to miss the great Stevie Lake."

Carole looked at her watch. "Gosh," she said. "I've got to hurry. Dad and I are driving over to the toy warehouse this afternoon to start our inventory."

"I've got to hurry, too," said Stevie, scraping up her remaining ice cream. "I've got my last voice lesson with Ms. Bennefield today."

"I've got to hurry, three," added Lisa. "Although not to anything fun. I've got to go home and help my mom." She sighed. "Today we're washing all the upstairs windows and baking shortbread."

The girls got up to pay their checks. "When shall we

ride again?" asked Lisa. "I can't wait to get out of the house already, and I'm not even there yet."

"Instead of riding, why don't you guys come over to my house tomorrow afternoon?" suggested Stevie. "I bought this awesome dress to wear when I sing the solo, and I'd like to try out my audition song on you. I've only sung it once for Alex, and he acted like he was going to throw up."

"Sure, Stevie." Carole smiled as she gave the waitress her money. "I'd love to."

"Me too," said Lisa. "It sounds like fun."

"Okay, then. Come over about three o'clock?"

"Great," said Carole as she put her coat on and pre- pared to go back into the frosty December air. "I'll see you guys tomorrow at Stevie's."

CAROLE LEFT TD's and hurried over to the bus stop, reaching it just as the bus pulled up and the doors opened. She climbed in, deposited her fare, and turned to find a seat. Usually the bus wasn't crowded on Saturday afternoon, but today was an exception. The seats were almost all filled by a noisy troop of Brownies on their way to see *The Nutcracker*. Carole was almost at the back of the bus before she found a spot to sit down.

"Whew," she breathed, falling into the seat as the bus lurched forward into the traffic. "I guess the closer it gets to Christmas the more hectic it gets."

She relaxed and looked out the window. *It really would be nice if it would snow this Christmas*, she thought, picturing everything coated in soft white powder. *We could take a trail ride in the snow, and then instead of a snowman, we could build a giant snow horse at the entrance of Pine Hollow.* The image brought a smile to her face. Then, suddenly, her smile turned to a frown. She had almost forgotten about the most important thing that had happened at Pine Hollow that day—the Secret Santas! What had Max said? Do some good deed for the person that they wouldn't ordinarily do for themselves? She pulled the slip of paper out of her pocket. LISA ATWOOD was spelled out in Max's squarish handwriting.

"Oh, brother," Carole whispered, frowning again. What could she possibly do for Lisa that Lisa wouldn't do for herself? And when on earth would she do it? She and Lisa were almost always together, and Lisa was the most well-organized person she knew. She always did her homework on time, she was never late on a science project, and she usually had the entire summer reading list read by the end of June. Carole sighed. There was nothing she could think to do for Lisa. Stevie, on the other hand, would have been easy. Anybody could do a hundred good deeds for Stevie that she would never get around to doing—like straightening up her cubby at Pine Hollow, or giving Belle's bridle a good saddle soaping. Carole shook her head. Whoever had drawn Stevie's name was going to have an easy time. Lisa was another matter entirely.

The bus veered around a corner, then rolled to its stop. Carole rose to get off. She would have to think about being a Secret Santa later. Right now she needed to get home and help her dad with a warehouse full of toys.

Colonel Hanson was waiting when Carole walked through their kitchen door. He had changed out of his khaki Marine Corps uniform and was wearing jeans and a green sweater.

"Hi, honey," he said, giving her a big hug. "How was Horse Wise today?"

"Well, it was an adventure," Carole said, remembering how she and Stevie had sneaked through the back door like spies. It seemed as if almost anything Stevie Lake was involved in was an adventure. Carole smiled up at her father's puzzled frown. "But we had a good time."

"You and Stevie weren't too late, were you?" he asked.

Carole shook her head. "We didn't miss anything really important."

"Good." Her father smiled. "Do you still want to help me with the inventory?"

"Absolutely," said Carole. "Just let me take a quick shower and change my clothes. I'll be ready in five minutes!"

She hurried upstairs. By the time she was dressed and ready to go, her father already had his coat on.

"How about we inventory for the rest of the afternoon, then drive over to Giuseppe's for a Hanson special?" her dad asked, jingling his car keys. A Hanson special was their favorite kind of pizza—half plain cheese, half pepperoni and mushroom.

"That sounds great, Dad. We haven't had one in a long time."

24

They got into their car and drove across town, turning down streets that were unfamiliar to Carole.

"Aren't the toys stored on the base, Dad?" she asked as her father drove along a street lined with old buildings that had broken windows and graffiti-painted walls.

"No, we didn't have room at Quantico this year, so we rented a place down here." Colonel Hanson pushed the button that automatically locked the doors of their car. "It's not a great area of town, but we got an old warehouse at a good price."

They drove on until they reached a large white building at one end of a street. The empty parking lot was littered with broken bottles, and a heavy chain and padlock hung across the front door.

"This is it," Colonel Hanson said. He smiled at Carole's puzzled frown. "I think you'll be very surprised when you go inside."

They got out of the car. From his pocket Colonel Hanson pulled the key chain on which he kept all his Marine Corps keys. He flipped through them, then grasped one bright blue key and fitted it into the lock. The key turned, and he pushed open the door. At first all Carole could see was darkness. Then her father turned on the lights.

"Gosh!" she gasped in amazement. The huge warehouse was filled with toys. There were dolls and games and balls and rocking horses. Brightly colored, soft toys for babies were stacked next to action figures for older children. Books and coloring books and drawing kits filled

25

one corner, while blocks and board games filled another. Carole blinked at all the bright colors. She'd never seen so many toys in her life!

"Gosh!" she repeated. "How long have the Marines been collecting these?"

"Well, it's a yearlong project," Colonel Hanson said with a chuckle. "We started right after last Christmas."

Carole blinked. She wouldn't know where to begin sorting through all these toys. "How are we supposed to do this, Dad?"

Colonel Hanson unzipped his briefcase and pulled out a thick computer printout. "This is a list of needy children and families the county human services agency sent us. We just have to inventory these toys and match them to the children on this list. You know, figure out what we have for boys under five, or for girls over eight. That kind of thing."

Carole still stared at the huge mounds of toys. "But, Dad, it'll take us months to do that, and it's only two weeks till Christmas."

"Oh, other Marines will work on this after hours during the week." Colonel Hanson smiled. "This is just the shift I chose because I thought it would be fun to do it together."

"That's a relief!" Carole cried. "For a minute I thought it was all up to just us."

Colonel Hanson looked at all the toys stacked around

26

the room and scratched his chin. "I've got an idea," he finally said. "Let's just pull all the baby toys we can find over in this one corner. Then we'll put all the toddler toys next to them, then the preschool toys next to them."

"Just like grades in school?" asked Carole.

"Right," said her father. "We'll go from youngest to oldest."

They started on the far wall of the warehouse, searching through all the boxes for toys for babies. After working a couple of hours, they had all of them piled in one corner of the building.

"Now," said Colonel Hanson, taping a sheet of paper that read BABIES to the tall stack. "On to the toddlers."

Again they looked through all the toys the Marines had gathered, now searching for toys that helped toddlers learn their colors and numbers. Carole found several new versions of some toys she'd had as a small child. In one corner, she found a doll exactly like one her mother had given her years ago.

"Look, Dad! Here's another Ahmarha."

Colonel Hanson came over and looked at the pretty little doll with her dark brown hair and cinnamon-colored skin. "I remember the day your mother gave you that doll," he said softly. "You had just begun to talk and you could barely say *doll*."

"Really?" Carole laughed.

Colonel Hanson nodded. "Your mother and I thought

you were the cutest little thing." He laughed. Then he saw a sad expression flicker across Carole's face. He put his arm around her. "You miss Mom a lot at Christmastime, don't you?"

Carole nodded. Her mother had died of cancer a few years ago, before she and Stevie and Lisa had started The Saddle Club. "I think about her a lot."

"I do, too," said Colonel Hanson, squeezing Carole's shoulder. "Sometimes I get real sad, but then I concentrate on all the wonderful things she did for us, and how much she loved to laugh. Remember that special Kwanzaa song she taught us?"

Carole nodded. " 'We bring to this feast of Karamu, our colors of Kwanzaa love,' " she sang.

Her father smiled. "Every time I feel sad about your mother at this time of year, I think of that song, and then I feel better." He gave Carole a hug. "Sometimes when we miss the people we love, all we need to do is think about something that was special to them—like a song, or something they thought was funny, and it's as if they're right here again, with us."

Carole hugged her father back. She thought of her mother often, in just the same way he did, and she, too, felt as if her mother was near. "I know exactly what you mean," she said.

"Then let's get back to work." Colonel Hanson smiled down at Carole. "I know your mother wouldn't want us to

28

goof off on this job. She would say it's much too important to get these toys distributed to the kids who need
them."

"Right," said Carole.

They worked for several more hours. Though there
weren't any clocks in the warehouse, Carole could tell by
the empty feeling in her stomach that it must be getting
close to suppertime.

"What time is it, Dad?" she finally asked.

Colonel Hanson looked at his watch. "Good grief!" he
cried. "It's almost eight o'clock! You must be starved."

"Well, I am getting a little hungry," Carole admitted.

"Gosh, honey, I had no idea it had gotten so late. I
guess we both got caught up in all this sorting."

They looked at the toys they had arranged in one corner. It was a lot, but it seemed to Carole that they had
made just the tiniest start.

"We'll quit now and let Captain Morton and her squad
take over tomorrow." Colonel Hanson made a check
mark on his list and began to put on his coat.

"It doesn't seem like we've done that much, Dad," Carole said. "And we've been here all afternoon."

Colonel Hanson looked at the toy-filled warehouse.
"We'll have troops working here all week, so by next
weekend we should be in good shape."

"Stevie and Lisa said they would help," Carole added.

"Great," said Colonel Hanson. "I knew I could rely on

The Saddle Club." He zipped up his jacket. "Are you ready for a Hanson special?"

"Oh, yes," said Carole. "I can smell it already. All that yummy cheese, all that delicious pepperoni."

Colonel Hanson grinned. "Okay, then. We'll lock up here, and then it's Giuseppe's, here we come!"

"LISA! DON'T CLIMB down yet. You've missed a spot!"

Lisa was standing on the next to the top rung of the stepladder from the garage. She'd spent most of the afternoon washing the upstairs windows in her house while her mother held the ladder to steady it. At the moment, her mother was still behind and below her, pointing to a tiny spot high on the inside of the top pane of glass.

"Where, Mom? I don't see it." Bright sunshine poured through the windowpane. Lisa couldn't see anything on the glass except her own reflection.

"It's right there, just over your left shoulder."

Lisa squinted at the glass. If she cocked her head in a certain direction, she could see a faint smudge of dirt that she'd missed with the paper towel. "That little thing?" She turned and looked down at her mother.

"Yes." Mrs. Atwood nodded. "It looks like a big blob from here."

Lisa squirted more window cleaner on the glass and rubbed it with the paper towel. The spot disappeared. "Is it gone now?" she asked, afraid to step down from the ladder for fear her mother would find another spot for her to scrub.

"I don't see it anymore." Mrs. Atwood peered up at the pane of glass. "Is this the last window in this room?"

"Yes," answered Lisa as she began to climb down. "This is the last window in the whole upstairs."

"Good," said Mrs. Atwood. "You've done a marvelous job, sweetie. Now if you'll put that ladder back in the garage we can start baking."

Lisa took a deep breath as her mother hurried downstairs to the kitchen. So far this afternoon they had cleaned out three closets, washed all the upstairs windows, and scrubbed the downstairs woodwork. And all to get ready for a bunch of people she could barely remember! Though she had a vague memory of what her cousins Douglas and Eliot looked like, the rest of the family was a blur, and now there were two more of them. "Darling twin girls," her mother had said. "Caitlin and Fiona."

With a sigh, Lisa began to fold up the ladder. She knew that her mother was a good mother, but sometimes she did get carried away about things. Usually she was very

32

concerned about redecorating the house or making sure Lisa had the right dancing lessons or drawing lessons to be a properly brought up young lady. But ever since Mrs. Atwood's cousin Sarah Ross had called in September, she'd been totally obsessed with planning their visit down to the last minute. Now that their arrival was drawing near, she had become a nonstop whirlwind of cooking, cleaning, and baking.

Lisa shook her head and listened as her mother started banging pots and pans around in the kitchen. Of all Christmases, why did the Rosses have to be coming this year? She had so much to do. First she needed to figure out what sort of good deed she could do for Max, whose name she had drawn at Horse Wise that morning. Max had lots of people helping him out all day, and most of the stuff he did, Lisa didn't know how to do, anyway. She couldn't give anybody a riding lesson, and she certainly didn't know how to manage some of the more difficult horses at the stable. There wasn't a thing she could think of that Max couldn't do better for himself.

"Lisa!" her mother called. "I need your help!"

"Okay. I'm coming." Lisa picked up the ladder. *Maybe I can think of a Secret Santa good deed while I bake shortbread,* she decided as she maneuvered the ladder down the stairs. *That way at least one part of my brain will be put to good use.*

By the time she had put the ladder back in the garage, Mrs. Atwood had the stove preheated and several pounds of butter softening. Lisa had to admit that it was nice to be in a warm kitchen after having been in the cold, damp garage, and the vanilla her mother was using for the shortbread made the room smell wonderful.

"All right, Lisa. Come over here and grease all our cookie sheets," Mrs. Atwood said. "But be sure and wash your hands first."

"Okay." Lisa went to the sink and turned on the water. The rush of bubbles reminded her of her other task: curing Prancer of her fear of water. *Wonder what Prancer would do if she saw this*, Lisa thought as she soaped her hands. *If one little creek freaks her out, a stream of rushing water would probably send her up a tree*. She rinsed her hands and sighed again. How on earth was she going to find the time to retrain Prancer before the Fairfax competition? She turned off the water and dried her hands. There was just too much to do this Christmas, and not nearly enough time.

She stooped down to get the cookie sheets out of the cabinet and noticed her mother studying the cookbook. "Have you ever made this before, Mom?"

"Yes, I've made shortbread before. I was just checking on the oven temperature. There are lots of other Scottish dishes I'm going to cook that are new to me, though." Mrs. Atwood smiled. "I'm going to try bannocks and clooty dumplings, and one night I'm going to fix haggis."

Lisa frowned. "Haggis?"

"Yes. It's practically the national dish of Scotland. It's

34

liver and suet and oatmeal and spices all tied up and boiled in a sheep's stomach."

Lisa frowned. Liver? Suet? Was her mother kidding? Already she could feel her stomach beginning to churn at the idea of haggis. Maybe the night her mother served haggis would be a good night to become a vegetarian!

"Aren't we going to have any American food while they're here?" she asked. "I mean, the Rosses are coming to America. They might want to try something like corn on the cob or sweet potatoes or pumpkin pie or barbecued ribs."

Mrs. Atwood measured several cups of flour into a big mixing bowl. "They might, but I think America will seem very big and strange to them. They're from a tiny village on the west coast of Scotland. I thought if I cooked them what they were used to eating there, they might feel more at home."

"Yes, but we are going to have our traditional Christmas dinner, aren't we?" Lisa began to rub shortening on a cookie sheet. "Pot roast with potatoes and peas?"

Mrs. Atwood shook her head. "Well, no, dear. This year I thought we might try salmon and wild rice."

"Salmon?" Lisa wrinkled her nose. "And rice? No pot roast and potatoes?"

Mrs. Atwood nodded. "Lisa, it's important that we make our guests feel at home. It's also important that they have a wonderful Christmas."

"How do Scottish people celebrate Christmas?" Lisa

asked in a shaky voice. *If these people eat liver cooked in a sheep's stomach, what in the world do they do on Christmas day—tie bells around a lamb's tail and chase him through the town?*

"Oh, I think they celebrate Christmas just the way we do—they decorate a tree and exchange gifts and go to church. Their cuisine is just a little different from ours."

"I'll say!" Lisa sprinkled flour on the greased cookie sheets. "Where are they all going to sleep?"

"Well, I thought I'd put James and Sarah in the guest room. Eliot and Douglas can sleep on the sofa bed in the den, and the twins—well, I'm not sure where we'll put the twins."

"Isn't that going to make things a little crowded?"

"Yes, it is. Look, sweetie. This year we're going to have to work together as a family. Sarah and James, of course, will take care of the twins. I'll be doing the cooking, and your father volunteered to make sure the house stayed clean. I thought maybe you could be in charge of entertaining Eliot and Douglas."

Lisa blinked. "But, Mom, I haven't talked or written to Eliot and Douglas in years. What do they like to do?"

"I don't know." Mrs. Atwood looked up from her mixing bowl. "Whatever Scottish boys like to do, I suppose. Eliot is fourteen and Douglas is thirteen. Play soccer, or maybe rugby. What's that sport where they slide stones on icy ponds? Curling?"

"Mom, there aren't that many icy ponds around here. And if we went out and started sliding stones across one, people would think we were crazy."

"Well, I'm sure there are other things you can do. You can take them to the movies or the shopping mall. They'd probably love Pine Hollow." Mrs. Atwood smiled.

"Do they wear regular clothes?" Lisa asked hesitantly.

"What do you mean, Lisa?" Mrs. Atwood was creaming butter and sugar together. "I'm sure Sarah dresses them delightfully."

"I mean do they wear jeans like regular kids, or do they wear kilts?" Lisa could just picture showing up at Pine Hollow with two teenage boys dressed in kilts. Everyone would laugh at her for the rest of her life!

"They don't wear kilts all the time over there," Mrs. Atwood assured her. "But they do wear them for special occasions." She stopped mixing the sugar and butter and smiled at Lisa. "The important thing is to be friendly and make sure the Rosses have a good time. They're spending a lot of money to come here and be with us."

"I know, Mom," Lisa said with a sigh.

She greased the last cookie sheet and sat down at the kitchen table. This was getting worse and worse. Now not only did she have to figure out what to do for Max and retrain Prancer not to fear crossing water, but she also had to distribute toys for the Marines and entertain her cousins from Scotland. Plus, according to her mother, they ate sheep guts, wore skirts, and played sports that she'd mostly never heard of. She'd played soccer at school, but rugby? And curling?

She sighed. This was going to be the strangest Christmas ever!

"GOLLY," HUFFED STEVIE as she pedaled her bike faster up the street. "I'm going to be late for this, too." It had been a less than perfect day for her from the beginning. First she'd overslept. Then she'd drawn snooty Veronica di-Angelo's name when Max passed around the Secret Santa helmet. And now, after she'd gotten back from TD's, the time had just slipped away and she was about to be late for her last voice lesson. Her only hope was that Ms. Bennefield's lessons tended to run overtime, so there was the slightest possibility that the student ahead of her might still be there.

She pedaled even faster. The cold air whistled past her ears. *Bicycles aren't nearly as efficient as horses*, she decided as she steered around a manhole cover. *Belle and I could*

39

*cut through these yards and jump the hedges. On a bicycle,
you have to stay on one side of the street.*

She zoomed around the last corner. Ms. Bennefield's
little redbrick house stood in the middle of the block.
Stevie could see the boy who took lessons before her getting into his mother's car. Ms. Bennefield was waving at
them as they pulled away from the curb.

"Thank heavens!" Stevie breathed. She pedaled furi-
ously the rest of the way down the street, then turned into
Ms. Bennefield's driveway. She squeezed on the brakes
and turned sideways to stop, throwing a fine spray of
gravel against Ms. Bennefield's garage.

"Goodness, Stevie, don't have a wreck!" Ms. Bennefield cried. "A voice lesson isn't worth breaking your
neck over."

"I know," said Stevie, gasping for breath. "But I've
been late for everything else today, and I wanted to get to
my last lesson on time."

Ms. Bennefield laughed. She had short auburn hair,
pretty green eyes, and a friendly smile. "Well, I just finished with my other student, so I would say you've timed
it perfectly. Come on in!"

Stevie parked her bike and followed her teacher inside.
Stevie had never seen a house quite like Ms. Bennefield's,
but she loved it. There was a huge grand piano in the
living room with a full-length mirror beside it. The walls
were filled with pictures of Ms. Bennefield in all the musi-

cals she'd been in, and there were several shots of her with movie stars. On the table across the room was a glittery headdress made out of fake bananas and coconuts that she'd worn in some Broadway play, and just behind the piano, on a tall perch, sat Tootie, Ms. Bennefield's gray cockatiel.

"Hi, Tootie," Stevie said, waving at the bird as she took off her coat and backpack.

"Hey, good-lookin'," croaked Tootie. "Merry Christmas!"

"Now, Tootie, you behave yourself," Ms. Bennefield scolded the bird, who just flapped his wings and let out an ear-piercing wolf whistle. She laughed and shook her head. "I almost had to cover him up during my last lesson. He seemed to think he could sing 'Ave Maria' better than my student could." Ms. Bennefield sat down at the piano, put on a pair of reading glasses, and studied her notes. "Okay, Stevie," she said. "Monday's your big audition, isn't it?"

Stevie nodded. "I'm so excited. I just know I'm going to get the part!"

"Have you been practicing all week?" asked Ms. Bennefield.

"Oh, yes." Stevie beamed. "This last month I've practiced my singing more than I've practiced my horseback riding."

"Well, let's do a few warm-ups and hear how you

sound." Ms. Bennefield played five notes. "Now, sing along with the piano, and remember to breathe the way I showed you!"

Stevie stood in front of the mirror and expanded her stomach muscles. At her first lesson Ms. Bennefield had explained that singing was a lot like riding a horse—you used the same muscles to sit on a horse that you did to push air through your vocal cords. Stevie had practiced hard every day on her breathing, but she still suspected that her stomach muscles were better at holding her up on Belle than they were at helping her sing a song.

"Okay, Stevie. Let me hear your E. One, two, three . . ."

"*Eeeeeeeeeeeeeeeeee.*" Stevie took a deep breath, opened her mouth, and sang. Tootie squawked once and cocked his head as if Stevie had produced a sound he'd never heard before.

"Good." Ms. Bennefield played on. "Tootie, be quiet. Stevie, try A."

"*Aaaaaaaaaaaaaaa,*" sang Stevie.

"Wonderful." Ms. Bennefield gave her a big smile. "Try to keep your jaw muscles loose. Now try I."

"*Iiiiiiiiiiii,*" sang Stevie. Then she started to giggle. "Sorry," she said when she saw Ms. Bennefield's puzzled expression. "That one always reminds me of Tarzan."

"It does, doesn't it?" Ms. Bennefield chuckled. "It sounds like you've been getting in some good practicing, though. Did you bring your music today?"

"Yes, it's right here." Stevie pulled three pieces of sheet music from her backpack and handed them to Ms. Bennefield.

"Have you decided which song you want to sing at your audition?"

" 'What Child Is This?', I think." Stevie liked all the songs Ms. Bennefield had assigned her, but she thought she sounded the best on "What Child Is This?" since it didn't go up quite so high as some of the others.

"Good choice," said Ms. Bennefield, studying the music. "It's a beautiful carol. Would you like to try it now?"

Stevie nodded. "I think I'm ready."

Ms. Bennefield arranged the music on her piano. "Okay. Now stand in front of the mirror and watch yourself as you sing. Concentrate on making a pleasant picture as well as a pleasant sound." She played an introductory chord as Stevie got into position.

"Remember what we've worked on. Stand up straight. Shoulders back, eyes alert and looking at your audience. Remember to breathe evenly, with your diaphragm. Keep your mouth and jaw relaxed, and try not to make faces. Remember, you're singing a song, not having a tooth drilled."

She sounds just like Max, Stevie thought as she tried to arrange herself in front of the mirror. She could just hear Max in the indoor ring saying, "Heels down, shoulders back, eyes soft, don't arch your back and remember to breathe!"

"Ready?" Ms. Bennefield played her beginning note on the piano.

Stevie nodded. She took a deep breath and opened her mouth, but instead of a perfect, pear-shaped note, out came a thunderous belch! Ms. Bennefield stopped playing in midnote, and Tootie squawked on his perch with alarm.

"Oh, Ms. Bennefield, I'm so sorry," Stevie cried, her face growing hot with embarrassment. "I didn't know I was going to do that. It must be the ice cream I just ate at TD's!"

Ms. Bennefield raised one eyebrow at Stevie, then began to laugh. "It's okay, Stevie. I was just expecting a B flat instead of a burp." She hit Stevie's note again. "Shall we take it from the top?"

Stevie nodded and resettled herself in front of the mirror. Ms. Bennefield began playing again. This time Stevie opened her mouth and actual notes came out. For a moment she felt as awkward as she usually did when she sang; then she remembered all the things Ms. Bennefield had told her to do. *Relax, smile, let the music bubble up from within you.* Suddenly the noise she was making actually began to sound pretty. She noticed that Ms. Bennefield was smiling as she played, and even Tootie seemed to listen, looking at her with his beady little eyes. Stevie sang all three verses of the song, and Ms. Bennefield finished with a flourish on the piano.

"Excellent, Stevie!" she cried. "You really have been working hard."

"Thanks." Stevie blushed with pleasure.

"There are just a few little areas where we need to do some work." Ms. Bennefield made some more notes on her music. "Let's take it from bar sixteen. You're going a little flat on the very last phrase."

Stevie took a deep breath and sang bar sixteen again. Thirty minutes later she was still standing in front of the mirror, still singing bar sixteen.

"Gosh," Stevie said when they had finished the twentieth rendition. "Learning to sing is just as hard as learning to ride."

"It really is, Stevie," Ms. Bennefield said. "Most people think you just open your mouth and this wonderful sound comes out, but singers have to practice constantly. It's very hard work." She smiled. "Would you like a glass of orange juice?"

"Is that okay to drink when you sing?" Stevie asked.

"Yes," said Ms. Bennefield. "Ice cream coats your vocal cords and makes your voice sound funny, so it's much better to drink water or orange juice. Come on in the kitchen and I'll pour you a glass."

Stevie followed Ms. Bennefield into her kitchen, which was almost as interesting as her living room. It was painted dark brown and more photographs lined the walls, but this time they were mixed in with *Playbills* from Broadway plays. A funny kind of Asian mask hung above the doorway, and a big papier-mâché Christmas tree stood on top of the refrigerator.

"Stevie, I know you've always wanted to be a good horsewoman, but when did you decide to become a good singer?" Ms. Bennefield asked as she poured a tall glass of orange juice.

"Well, I've always liked to sing, but I guess I really got interested in sounding good when Mr. Vance took over our drama program at school. He's a super-neat teacher, and when he announced the auditions for this Christmas play, I really wanted to try out."

"Oh?" Ms. Bennefield handed Stevie her juice.

"Yes. There's this other girl who's trying out for the part, too. Only she's this big snobby jerk who thinks just because she's rich she can do everything."

Ms. Bennefield frowned. "Does she sing, too?"

Stevie took a swallow of orange juice and nodded. "Only she sounds like a sick cat when she goes up high."

"Well." Ms. Bennefield laughed. "You certainly don't sound like that." She gave Stevie a warm smile. "I'm really proud of the way you've worked, Stevie. Not everybody is blessed with a beautiful voice, but everybody can improve their singing, and you've certainly done that."

"Thanks," Stevie said as she finished her juice.

"Shall we go through your song one more time?" asked Ms. Bennefield.

"Sure," said Stevie.

They returned to the living room, where Tootie was

waiting on his perch. Ms. Bennefield took her seat at the piano while Stevie stood in front of the mirror.

"Okay." Ms. Bennefield played an arpeggio. "Here's your intro."

Stevie took a deep breath, listened for her cue, and began to sing. All of a sudden her voice came effortlessly out of her mouth. She hit every note perfectly, she stayed in time with the music, and at the very end, where she'd kept going flat, she stayed right on the pitch. As the song ended, her voice and Ms. Bennefield's piano seemed to blend together perfectly.

"*Baaaarrrrkkkk!*" Tootie's squawk broke the silence. "Bravo!" he screeched. "Encore! Merry Christmas!"

"Oh, Tootie," Ms. Bennefield cried. "You're absolutely right! That was wonderful!" She got up from the piano and gave Stevie a big hug. "I am so proud of you!"

Stevie hugged her back. "I did sound pretty good, didn't I?"

"You sounded the best you ever have," Ms. Bennefield said. "If you sing like that Monday, I'm sure you'll get the part!"

"Wow, Ms. Bennefield, thanks."

It was time to go. Stevie gathered up her music and stuffed it into her backpack. "Thanks for everything. I wouldn't be half this good if it wasn't for you."

"You did it yourself, Stevie," Ms. Bennefield said, helping Stevie on with her coat. "You were determined to do it, and you practiced hard and concentrated."

"Do you really think I'll do okay on Monday?" Stevie asked as she opened Ms. Bennefield's front door.

"I think you'll do fine. Just breathe with your diaphragm, and if you get nervous before the audition, remember to do your lip rolls."

"Is that where you blow bubbles underwater, only there's no water?" Stevie stepped out into the frosty air.

"Right," said Ms. Bennefield. "That will help keep your mouth and jaw relaxed." She watched as Stevie shouldered her backpack and got on her bicycle. "Bye, Stevie," she called. "Good luck on Monday. Let me know what happens."

"I will, Ms. Bennefield," Stevie called as she pedaled off. "Thanks for all your help."

6

"HI, CAROLE!" LISA called as her friend got off the bus. Lisa had phoned Carole earlier that day and they had agreed to meet at the bus stop and walk to Stevie's house together. It was Sunday afternoon, and both girls were eager to hear Stevie's new, improved singing voice.

"Hi, Lisa." Carole pulled her red knitted cap lower over her ears. "Are you ready for the big performance?"

"I can hardly wait!" Lisa replied. "I just hope Stevie really sounds as good as she thinks she does."

"Me too," agreed Carole with a slight wince. "Otherwise it could be a real disaster." Carole and Lisa had heard Stevie sing many times. Though she always sang with great gusto, her crooning had definitely been off-key.

"Well, maybe all these voice lessons have turned her into a real virtuoso," said Lisa hopefully.

"I think it would take more than voice lessons to turn Stevie into a virtuoso," Carole said as the girls walked toward Stevie's house. "I think it would take more like a miracle."

They walked down the street, looking at all the Christmas decorations people had put on their houses. One house had a huge gold wreath on the front door, while another was covered in tiny white lights that twinkled constantly.

"Boy, it's pretty this time of year," said Lisa.

"I know." Carole smiled at the bright decorations. "If only it would snow."

Lisa buttoned the top button of her coat against the chilly air. "Hey, how did your toy drive work go yesterday?"

"Great," said Carole. "Dad and I worked till eight o'clock sorting through all the baby toys and toddler toys. There's still a ton more to do, though."

"Will you get it done in time for Christmas?" Lisa asked.

"I'm sure we will. Other Marines are volunteering their time at night." Carole looked at Lisa. "Do you think you'll be able to help us distribute the toys when it gets closer to Christmas?"

"Unless I'm dead from helping my mother get ready for our company," said Lisa with a sigh. "We worked all afternoon and into the night. I've never baked so much shortbread before in my life. We've got enough to feed an army, and now my mother's baking some kind of dumpling stuff!" Lisa didn't mention the awful haggis dish they were supposed to eat—she was afraid Carole might throw up right there on the side of the road.

"Maybe Scottish people have big appetites," Carole said.

"I hope they do," replied Lisa. "Otherwise we'll be eating this stuff for the next three years!"

They turned down Stevie's driveway. The Lakes' house was decorated for the holidays as well, with tiny lights glittering on the bushes next to the porch and a big green wreath with a red bow on the front door.

"Looks like the Lakes are ready for Christmas," Carole said as she rang the doorbell and sniffed the fragrant pine wreath.

"I think the Lakes are ready for everything." Lisa giggled. "At least I know Stevie is."

After a moment the big front door swung open. Chad, Stevie's older brother, stood there, dressed in a warm-up suit, the earphones of a portable CD player plugged into his ears. He smiled when he saw Lisa and Carole and unplugged himself from the music.

"Hi," he said. "Come on in."

"Hi, Chad." Lisa and Carole stepped into the warm living room, where a fire crackled in the fireplace. "Is Stevie here?"

"She's upstairs practicing her singing." Chad rolled his eyes. "Which is why I'm down here plugged into Shimmery Emery. Everybody else has gone shopping. Nobody can stand the noise."

Carole and Lisa gave each other a worried glance. They knew how important singing this solo had become to Stevie. "Is it really that bad?" Carole asked Chad softly.

Chad made a terrible face. "Go upstairs and listen for yourself."

He plugged back into the CD and went into the den while Carole and Lisa took off their coats and tiptoed upstairs. They didn't hear any shrieking or off-key singing, so they went to Stevie's room and knocked on her door.

The door flew open. Stevie stood there, grinning. "Hi!" she said. "I was just trying on my new dress while I was waiting for you guys to show up. Come on in and tell me what you think."

Carole and Lisa stepped in and closed the door behind them. Stevie stood in the middle of the room and modeled the dress by twirling in a tight circle, holding the skirt out. "Well," she laughed. "Am I gorgeous or what?"

Lisa and Carole blinked at Stevie. Her dress was a beautiful emerald green velvet that made her hazel eyes sparkle. Her shoulder-length hair looked blonder against the dark green of the dress, and her complexion had a wonderful rosy glow.

"Stevie!" Lisa gasped. "You look beautiful!"

"You certainly do," agreed Carole, her eyes wide.

"Well, it's not as comfortable as jeans and a sweatshirt,

but for a dress, it's not too bad." Stevie smiled. "I think Phil will really be impressed when the curtains open and there I am, singing a solo in this."

"Stevie, have you gotten the part for sure yet?" Carole asked gently.

"No, but I know I will. Mr. Vance really likes me. And after all my voice lessons I sound great. And the only other person trying out for the solo is Veronica, and I've told you how bad she sounds." Stevie grinned. "Sit down and I'll sing my song for you."

Lisa and Carole plopped onto Stevie's bed while Stevie rummaged in her backpack for her music.

"This is what I've decided to sing tomorrow," she said, pulling out a sheet of music. "Ms. Bennefield thinks it's a good choice."

Lisa and Carole each secretly crossed their fingers and waited for Stevie to begin. She stood before them, cleared her throat, took a deep breath, and started to sing.

" 'What child is this, who laid to rest in Mary's lap is sleeping?' " Stevie crooned.

Lisa and Carole glanced at each other. This was amazing! Stevie actually didn't sound too bad!

" 'Whom angels greet with anthems sweet while shepherds watch are keeping?' " Stevie sang on. Lisa and Carole could hardly believe their ears. What was Chad talking about? This was actually very good. Stevie sounded a thousand percent better!

" 'This, this—' "

Just as Stevie's voice began to climb higher, a thunderous *"Stevie!"* roared up from downstairs.

Stevie stopped singing and opened the door. "What do you want, Chad?" she shrieked down the staircase. "I was singing!"

"You've got a phone call!" Chad bellowed. "I've been yelling at you for five minutes!"

"Okay, okay," called Stevie, closing the door. "Thanks." She dropped down on her hands and knees and fished her phone out from under her bed. "Hang on," she said to Carole and Lisa. "I'll finish my song in a minute."

She picked up the receiver. "Hello?"

"Stevie?" It was a familiar voice but one she didn't often hear on the phone. She tried to place it, but then the voice placed itself. "It's Veronica."

"DiAngelo?" Stevie asked.

"Of course," Veronica said. "Do you know another Veronica?"

It occurred to Stevie to say it was a good thing she didn't, but that wouldn't exactly be in the spirit of Christmas. Instead, she said, "No, but I wasn't expecting to hear from you, that's all."

"Well, did you hear from Mr. Vance?"

"No, what about? Why would he call me?"

"Well, then how about Miss Fenton?"

The only times Stevie ever heard from Miss Fenton were when she was in trouble. She couldn't for the life of

54

her think of anything she'd done recently that Miss Fenton would need to talk to her about, except maybe for the fact that she'd used all the paper towels in the girls' room to prop up the leg on the broken couch in the library, but she was sure nobody had seen her do it, and besides, using paper towels was better than using a book, right?

"Miss Fenton? No. I haven't heard anything."

"Well, the way I heard it, she's steaming mad," Veronica said.

Now Stevie was curious. Miss Fenton might be *irritated* by a pile of paper towels, but not steaming mad. This was something else altogether.

"It has to do with Cross Academy, I guess." Cross Academy was a nearby private school and Fenton Hall's archrival. They played each other in every sport, and every time Fenton played Cross, it was a big deal. All week Fenton's hallways had been plastered with posters about how Fenton Hall should CROSS OUT CROSS in the basketball game to be played at Cross next week.

"Huh?" Stevie asked. This wasn't making any sense at all, and she couldn't imagine why Veronica was calling her.

"I can understand why you wouldn't want to say anything," said Veronica.

"About what?" Stevie demanded.

"The basketballs, of course."

If Stevie had been confused before, she was dumbfounded now.

"Veronica, I really have no idea what you're talking about." She rolled her eyes to let Lisa and Carole know that, one way or another, Veronica was being Veronica.

"Of course," Veronica said in her most condescending tone.

Stevie was inches from simply slamming down the phone, but her curiosity was piqued. "Tell me about the basketballs," she said.

"Well, not that you would know anything about this, Stevie, but the way I hear it, somebody—and nobody knows exactly who, but it must be one of those people who are always getting into trouble—*somebody* got into the athletic supply closet at Cross Academy and punctured every single one of their basketballs!"

"Who would do something like that?" Stevie blurted out.

"Exactly!" said Veronica.

Then it began to sink in. Veronica thought Stevie had done it. No way. Stevie was more than capable of pranks. She'd be the first to admit it, and maybe even say it proudly. She was even capable of slightly mean pranks—especially when it came to her brothers—but she was in no way capable of such a totally mean and destructive prank.

But if Veronica thought she did it, who else might? Miss Fenton? Stevie felt a terrible knot in her stomach.

"Anyway," said Veronica, "I guess Miss Fenton has announced that she's going to be in the auditorium between four and five tomorrow, and the person who did it is supposed to come forward and confess, which might, just *might* save them from being drawn and quartered by Miss Fenton and Mr. Lord, the headmaster at Cross."

"So, what about our auditions?" Stevie asked.

"Well, they can't be in the auditorium at *four* o'clock, can they?" Veronica answered.

"No, I guess not."

"Just thought you'd want to know," said Veronica.

"Uh, thanks," said Stevie. And she hung up.

"What was that about?" Carole asked.

"It was Veronica gloating," said Stevie, and she explained to Lisa and Carole about the basketballs. "She thinks I'm going to be in big trouble, but I didn't have anything to do with that. I mean, I hope Fenton beats Cross and all, but I certainly don't care enough to get into trouble over it."

"You'd never do anything like that," Lisa said.

"Well, you know that and I know that, but apparently Veronica doesn't, and I can't be absolutely certain that Miss Fenton doesn't, either."

"So what are you going to do?"

"Well, first of all, I'm not going to utter the word *basketball* tomorrow. I don't want anybody at that school connecting me with that mean and crude prank. And the next thing I'm definitely going to do is to stay far, far away from the auditorium tomorrow afternoon between four and five. The auditions have been changed to five o'clock."

"Is that what Veronica said?" Lisa asked.

"Well, they can't be before because there are some classes until four, and they can't be anyplace but the auditorium, so they have to be at five o'clock. I'll wait in the library. It's the last place Miss Fenton would think to look for me. Shall I finish my song now?"

"Oh, yes, Stevie, please go ahead. You sound wonderful!" Carole said.

"You really do, Stevie. You've improved tremendously. I just know Mr. Vance will give you the solo," added Lisa.

"Just think." Stevie grinned before she started to sing. "This could be the start of my second-greatest career!"

"What's your first-greatest career, Stevie?" asked Carole. "Riding horses or getting into trouble?"

"Riding horses, of course." Stevie laughed. "Trouble just seems to happen on its own."

THE NIGHT OF the play had finally arrived. Excitement crackled through the auditorium as everyone waited for the lights to go down. "Gosh," said Phil Marsten to his friend A.J. "I wonder what part Stevie is playing in this."

"It couldn't be a singing role," said A.J., settling down in his seat beside Phil. "I've heard Stevie sing before."

"I know what you mean," replied Phil. "But she said I'd be really surprised."

The lights dimmed and the curtain rose. Phil gasped. There, standing all alone onstage, was his girlfriend, Stevie Lake. She was dressed in the most beautiful green dress he'd ever seen. She flashed a gorgeous smile at the audience. Then, with the slightest nod to her accompanist, she began to sing.

Phil's jaw dropped. "That's Stevie!" he cried. "And she's singing like an angel!"

"Stevie!"

"Huh?" Stevie looked up from the breakfast table. Her mother stood in front of her, holding two boxes of cereal.

"Do you want cornflakes or granola this morning? I've already asked you twice. You're just sitting there like you're a million miles away."

"She's daydreaming about her play," Stevie's twin brother, Alex, teased. "She's thinking how beautifully she'll sing, all for Phil."

"Daydreaming about singing something beautiful sure beats sitting here listening to you," Stevie snarled back.

"Stevie and Alex," Mrs. Lake said with a note of warning in her voice. "It's Monday morning, a short time before Christmas. Let's try to show a little holiday spirit toward each other." She shook both cereal boxes again. "Stevie? Cornflakes or granola?"

"Granola, Mom," Stevie decided. "Thanks," she added as her mother poured cereal into her bowl.

"What time is your audition, Stevie?" Mr. Lake asked, looking at her over his newspaper.

"Five," said Stevie. "Mr. Vance changed it from four."

Mr. Lake frowned. "Hmmm, it'll be dark by then. Would you like me to stop by Fenton Hall on my way home from the office and give you a ride home?"

"Sure, Dad, that would be great." Stevie smiled as she poured milk over her cereal.

"Well, if you guys want a ride to school, we've got to leave in thirty seconds." Mrs. Lake took off the apron that covered her crisp gray business suit and glanced at her watch. "I've got to be downtown in court in half an hour, and I've got just enough time to drop you off."

Stevie finished her breakfast in four bites, then joined her three brothers in putting on their coats and piling into Mrs. Lake's station wagon. Michael, Stevie's youngest brother, managed to turn one of his pet white mice loose in the front seat, but by the time they rolled up in front of school, he had recaptured it.

"Bye, you guys," Mrs. Lake said as her children scrambled out of the car. "Have a good day! Hey, Stevie," she called as Stevie closed the door. "Break a leg at your audition!"

"Break a leg?" Stevie frowned. Why would her mother want her to break her leg?

"It's theater lingo," Mrs. Lake said with a laugh. "It means good luck. I just know you'll be great!"

"Thanks, Mom." Stevie smiled. "See you tonight."

The school day crept by for Stevie. Everyone was talking about the basketball prank. Stevie shut her ears to all conversations on the topic and, true to her word, didn't mention the word *basketball* all day.

All she could think about was the audition that afternoon. Instead of memorizing the Bill of Rights in history class, she tried to remember all the relaxation techniques Ms. Bennefield had showed her. In algebra class she concentrated on whole and quarter notes instead of negative numbers, and at lunch she ate a piece of chocolate cake instead of her usual ice cream.

Finally, as the hands of the clock reached three, the dismissal bell rang. The rest of her science class raced toward the door, but Stevie got up slowly and walked out into the hall. She climbed the stairs to the second floor, where the library was. *I can get my homework done and kill two hours at the same time*, she thought.

The library was just as deserted as the classrooms. Stevie tossed her books on a table by the window and sat down so that she could both watch the clock and look at what was going on outdoors. She checked the time. It was ten past three. Almost two hours to go. She sighed and opened her history book. She might as well read that night's assignment.

By the time the clock read five past four, she'd read her history, done her science, and worked several pages ahead in her algebra. Again she sighed. Why had Mr. Vance moved the auditions back so late? Didn't he realize there was nothing for anybody to do here when school wasn't in session?

She turned and looked out the window. A boy on a bicycle rode across the soccer field, his dog following him. Stevie thought of pets, which made her think of Belle. Then she thought of Pine Hollow and Max. Then she jumped. She had completely forgotten about the Secret Santas, and she had drawn Veronica diAngelo's name!

"Yikes!" she said out loud. "What can I do to—um, er, I mean *for* her?" Stevie knew Veronica was going to be furious when Mr. Vance gave her this solo, and getting a Secret Santa good deed from Stevie on top of that might make her even madder. *Maybe I ought to just forget about being a Secret Santa*, Stevie thought, frowning. No, that wouldn't be right. She would have to do something really super-duper nice for Veronica. That would make Veronica feel a whole lot better about everything.

Stevie sat back in her chair and tapped her pencil on the table. But what could she do for Veronica? Veronica already managed to get Red O'Malley to do most of her chores for her horse, Danny, so that wouldn't be any big surprise. And whenever the Pine Hollow riders had a clean-up-the-stables day, Veronica usually had some important appointment with her hairdresser or her Italian tutor. There was nothing she needed or wanted that Stevie could do for her.

"Hmmmm," Stevie said. This was going to take some thought. She had just begun to wonder whether Veronica's fancy dressage saddle might need some extra cleaning, when she looked at the clock. Where had the time gone? It was quarter to five!

Golly, she thought, *I'd better get going*. She gathered her books and hurried down to the bathroom. It was dark. She turned on the lights and looked at herself in the mirror. She looked okay. Maybe a little pale, but that was to be expected at her first audition. She closed her eyes and tried to remember everything Ms. Bennefield had taught her. *Blow bubbles to keep your lips loose, breathe with your stomach, smile, shrug your shoulders up and down to stay relaxed.* Stevie did all those exercises for five minutes; then it was time to go. She pulled her music out of her backpack, grabbed her coat, and ran down the stairs to the auditorium. She absolutely could not be late for this. Mr. Vance would have a fit!

When she bounded down the stairs and turned the corner, she found the auditorium door closed. *That's odd*, she thought. Mostly kids come and go a lot when a play practice starts. She walked over to the door and listened. That was even more odd. Someone was playing the piano, and someone else was singing!

And there was something odder still. The auditorium was right across the hall from Miss Fenton's office. Stevie could hear the rise and fall of an angry voice coming from there—the unmistakable tones of Miss Fenton's fury. She had her suspects in custody right where she wanted them, in her own office.

A knot formed in Stevie's stomach with the realization that she'd been had, but good, by Veronica diAngelo. Miss Fenton was angry, all right; she'd waited for the basketball hooligans to confess, all right; it had been at four o'clock, all right; but it hadn't been in the auditorium. She'd been in her own office the whole time, just as Stevie had been in the library the whole time.

Trembling with dread, Stevie opened the auditorium

door, knowing before she saw it exactly what would greet her. There, onstage, was the entire cast of the play, and right in the middle, singing in a lime-colored spotlight, was Veronica diAngelo!

The door slammed shut behind Stevie. The music stopped. Everyone looked at her.

"What's going on?" Stevie asked, still not believing what she was seeing. She hurried down to Mr. Vance at the piano. "Aren't we having auditions for the solo today?"

Mr. Vance's eyebrows rose. "We did have them, Stevie. At four o'clock. We waited for you until four-fifteen, and then we had to go on with the rehearsal. I gave the solo to Veronica, who was here on time."

"But I thought the auditions were at five," Stevie began, blinking back tears of fury and disappointment.

"Sorry, Stevie." Mr. Vance shook his head. "It was four. I announced it clearly at the end of rehearsal on Friday afternoon. As I recall, you were staring out the window with your sheet music on your lap."

The room grew silent. Everyone in the auditorium was staring at Stevie, waiting to see what she was going to do. Veronica smiled weakly from the center of the stage and shrugged. Stevie glared at her. Had she called her the day before on purpose to confuse her? It was possible, but it was just as possible that Veronica had been mixed up, too. Stevie took a deep breath. As much as she wanted to accuse Veronica of cheating in front of Mr. Vance and the whole cast, she said nothing. There was no way she could prove it, and the whole argument would only wind up being her word against Veronica's.

Mr. Vance finally broke the heavy silence. "Let's take five, everybody!"

The cast scurried out of their positions. Veronica exited stage left, as far away from Stevie as she could get. Stevie stood there in stunned silence. All her work and practice with Ms. Bennefield had come to nothing. She'd never even gotten a chance to try out. Now Phil would never hear her sing onstage. Neither would her family, or her friends, or Ms. Bennefield, or anybody. Again hot tears began to sting her eyes.

"Come over here, Stevie," Mr. Vance called softly from the piano. "I want to talk to you."

She walked over to him. They both hopped up on the stage and let their legs dangle over the edge.

"Look, Stevie, I know how hard you've worked on your singing, and I'm really proud of you for that. But you also need to work hard on paying attention in class. If I let you try out for the solo now, it wouldn't be fair to Veronica, who was here at the proper time." Mr. Vance took his glasses off and smiled. "There's a spot, though, in the chorus where I could use another singer. Would you like to do that?"

Stevie sighed and shrugged. As much as she wanted to please Mr. Vance, she felt as if Veronica had stolen something from her, and to be in the chorus would somehow

66

be like letting Veronica know it was okay. Only in this case it wasn't okay at all.

"Why don't you go home and give it some thought?" Mr. Vance put his arm around her and squeezed her shoulders. "You're one of my best troupers, and I want you to be in all our plays."

"I'll think about it," said Stevie. She hopped down off the stage and started to put her coat on.

"And, Stevie, don't forget that this spring we'll be doing *Once Upon a Mattress*." Mr. Vance smiled. "I can think of one role in that play that would be perfect for you."

"Really?" asked Stevie. "Which one?"

"Winnifred, the princess," said Mr. Vance with a wink. "It's the lead."

"Gosh, Mr. Vance, thanks for telling me," she said. She zipped up her jacket. "I'll let you know about the chorus part. Right now, though, I need to go wait for my dad."

"Why don't you go out through the backstage door?" said Mr. Vance. "That way you won't have to walk all the way around the building."

"Okay." Stevie threaded her way through the heavy curtains as she heard Mr. Vance play a chord on the piano and call everybody back to their places. Backstage she could hear Veronica beginning her solo. Stevie felt anger beginning to boil up inside her all over again.

She saw a big cardboard box she'd never seen before. It was on a chair, and the words SOLO COSTUME were lettered on top. Stevie frowned. Nobody had ever mentioned that singing the solo also involved wearing a costume.

She walked over to the box and peered inside. It was hard to tell what the costume was, so she put her books down and reached into the box. First she pulled out a long, brown pajama-looking thing; then she pulled out four shoelike pieces that looked sort of like hooves.

"What on earth is this supposed to be?" she whispered as she peered deeper into the box. She held the pajamas and the hooves in one hand and reached for the final piece. She pulled it from the darkness of the box and held it up to the light.

"Oh, my gosh!" she said, giggling with delight. She was holding the head of a donkey costume! It was brown felt with huge long ears that stood straight up. Stevie laughed until tears came to her eyes when she realized what was going to happen. Veronica, who had wanted this solo more than anything else in the world, so badly that she'd been willing to lie, cheat, and steal for it, was going to have to sing it dressed like a donkey!

Quietly Stevie put the costume back in the box. She knew Veronica didn't know about this—otherwise she would never have been so determined to get the part. Stevie wondered if Mr. Vance was going to break the news to her this afternoon. It would almost be worth hanging around to see the expression on the other girl's face. But then Stevie remembered her father sitting outside waiting for her.

"I guess I'd better go," she whispered as she closed the box. She gathered her books again and walked to the backstage door. Even though it would be hard to tell her family that she hadn't gotten the solo because she'd been mixed up on the time, at least she wouldn't have to stand in front of Phil and all her friends to sing dressed like a donkey!

"LISTEN!" CAROLE CRIED as she and her father walked up their front steps. "The phone's ringing!" The Hansons had just come back from working at the toy warehouse, and the phone had begun to ring the moment they reached their front door.

"Somebody must really want to talk to us." Carole listened to the phone's insistent ringing as her father unlocked the door.

"Oh, it's probably somebody selling something," Colonel Hanson said. "Lightbulbs or carpet cleaning."

"I don't know, Dad." Carole frowned. "That phone's got a funny ring to it."

"A funny ring?" Colonel Hanson shook his head as he opened the door. "Hurry on in, then. Maybe you can grab it before they hang up."

Carole dashed into the living room and down the hall. "Hello?" she gasped, grabbing the phone on its tenth ring.

"Carole! Where have you been?" Stevie's voice came over the receiver.

"I've been helping my dad at the toy warehouse, Stevie. We worked there all afternoon and just walked in the door. I haven't even taken off my coat." Carole frowned again. Something in Stevie's voice didn't sound right. "Is something wrong?"

"Yes, a lot's wrong." Stevie's voice cracked. "Take off your coat and call me back. I need to tell you something important."

"Okay," said Carole. "I'll call you back in five minutes."

She hung the phone up and took off her coat. "That was Stevie on the phone, Dad."

"I guess you were right about that funny ring, then," Colonel Hanson said from the kitchen, chuckling. "Go ahead and call her back if you want. I'm heating up some soup for supper. We'll eat in about half an hour."

Carole hurried to her room and sat down on her bed. *Uh-oh,* she thought as she punched Stevie's number. Stevie must have auditioned for the solo and not gotten the part. The phone only rang once before Stevie answered.

"Carole, is that you?"

"Yes."

"Just a minute," Stevie said. "Let me click Lisa on and we can all talk together."

There were two clicks, and Lisa's voice came on the line. "Hi, everybody."

"Hi, Lisa," Carole replied.

"Okay, you guys, listen up." Stevie took command of the conversation. "You won't believe what happened to me this afternoon."

"What?" Lisa and Carole asked together.

"Remember yesterday, when Veronica called and told me that the audition had been changed to five instead of four?"

"Yes."

"Well, I sat through school all day today. Then I killed two hours in the library, just waiting for the rehearsal to begin. Finally it was time to go down to the auditorium. I got out my music, did my breathing exercises, and hurried down there, and guess what!"

"What?" asked Lisa and Carole.

"Veronica was standing in the middle of the stage, already singing my solo!" Stevie's voice was shrill with anger.

"How come?" Carole was shocked. She knew Stevie still wasn't the greatest singer in the world, but she had thought that Mr. Vance would at least let her try out for the solo.

"That's exactly what I asked Mr. Vance. He said the audition had started at four, just like I'd thought it did.

72

He said he waited until four-fifteen for me to show up, but then he had to go ahead and start the rehearsal, so he gave the part to Veronica." Stevie sounded again as if she might cry.

"Stevie, that's awful!" said Lisa.

"I know." Stevie's voice trembled. "All that practice and I never even got a chance to try out!"

"Do you think Veronica called and got you confused on purpose?" asked Carole.

Stevie didn't answer for a long moment. "I don't know," she finally said. "I know Veronica's awfully spoiled and mean, but I just can't believe she would be that dishonest!"

"If Veronica really did that, it would be worse than cheating on a final exam!" breathed Lisa.

"I know," Stevie said. "But I can't prove it. It's just my word against hers."

"But it does seem kind of funny that she managed to get there on time and you didn't," Carole pointed out.

"Exactly," agreed Stevie. "It seems a little too funny to be true, doesn't it?"

"Oh, Stevie!" Carole cried. "It's about the lowest thing I've ever heard of anybody doing."

"I know." Stevie took a deep breath, as if she was trying hard not to cry. "But let me tell you the rest of the story," she added, suddenly sounding happier. "Mr. Vance said I could go out through the backstage door and meet my dad. While I was walking through all the props backstage I saw this box marked 'Solo Costume.' I looked inside, and guess what!"

"What?" Again Carole and Lisa spoke together.

"Veronica's going to have to sing her solo dressed up like a donkey!"

"No!" Lisa squealed with delight.

"Yes!" cried Stevie. "It's this awful-looking brown pajama thing that has four detachable hooves and a headpiece that covers everything but your face! Plus, it's got these two huge ears! But the best part about it is that Veronica thinks she's going to be singing in a really pretty dress. She has no idea she's going to have to dress up like a donkey!"

"Oh, Stevie," Carole and Lisa said as they burst out laughing together. "That's too good to be true!"

"I know," cackled Stevie. "I just wish I could have seen her face when Mr. Vance showed her what she was going to have to wear."

For a few minutes all the girls could do was laugh at the idea of Veronica singing in a donkey costume. Then, when everyone had calmed down, Stevie spoke again.

"I don't know if Veronica did this on purpose or not, but she sure looked guilty when I walked in the door."

"Really?" Carole could just imagine the look on Veronica's face.

"Yes, she did," said Stevie. "I've been thinking about it all night, and I think Veronica deserves a major Pine Hollow revenge."

"What did you have in mind, Stevie?" Lisa had never heard such determination in Stevie's voice.

"I don't know yet," Stevie replied. "I'll have to give something of this magnitude a lot of thought."

"Wait a minute, Stevie," cautioned Carole. "Don't you see the joke's already on Veronica? She's gone to all this trouble and maybe even cheated, only to have to spend her big moment wrapped up in a donkey costume. Everybody will be in hysterics! That's poetic justice enough!"

"Well, maybe," Stevie admitted. "I would still like to plot something that would teach her the lesson of her life!"

"I've got an idea," said Lisa. "Why don't we meet at Pine Hollow tomorrow after school and take a trail ride? Stevie, that'll give you time to cool off. You can get a chance to think about what you should do to Veronica, and I'll get a chance to get out. I haven't done anything since yesterday afternoon except go to school and clean house for our company!"

"Well, maybe a ride in the country would make me feel a little better," Stevie admitted.

"I think that's a great idea," said Carole. "But I can't take a long ride. My dad and I are scheduled to do some more inventory tomorrow evening."

"Then let's meet at the stable and take the creek trail," Lisa suggested. "It's shorter, and I can see if Prancer's calmed down about crossing water."

"Okay. Then I'll see you guys tomorrow," said Stevie.

"Right. And, Stevie, don't be too upset about this. Lisa and I heard you sing yesterday, and we thought you were great," Carole said.

"Yes, Stevie. You'll get lots of other solos, for sure."

"Thanks, guys, for trying to make me feel better. I'll see you tomorrow."

THE NEXT AFTERNOON the girls met at Pine Hollow. The whole place was buzzing with activity. Mrs. Reg, Max's mother, was telling Red O'Malley where to store some new saddle pads, while Deborah, Max's wife, paced around with a cell phone glued to her ear. Max was trying to give an adult lesson in the indoor ring with baby Maxi riding on his shoulders.

"Wow," said Lisa as she and Carole walked toward their horses' stalls. "This place is like a three-ring circus!"

"I know." Carole dodged out of Red's way as he unpacked the new saddle pads. "It seems like everything gets busier at Christmas."

"It certainly does at my house," replied Lisa. "I don't think my mother's turned the stove off in three days. We have so many Scottish pastries in the freezer we could probably open the Loch Ness Take-out."

Carole laughed. "Are Scottish pastries as good as Danish pastries?"

"Who knows?" Lisa said. "My dad and I are too busy cleaning to try any."

The girls turned the corner. Stevie stood at Belle's stall, brushing her silky forelock.

"Hi, Stevie!" the girls called.

"Hi, Carole." Stevie gave them a thin smile. "Hi, Lisa."

"How was school today?" Carole asked as they came closer. She noticed that Stevie's eyes looked puffy, as if she'd been crying. "Any apologies from you-know-who?"

Stevie shook her head. "None at all. Today she strutted around like normal. Yesterday afternoon on the stage she really looked scared."

"She probably was scared, Stevie," Lisa said. "She was probably terrified of what you were going to do to her."

"Well, she ought to just stay scared, as far as I'm concerned." Stevie frowned as she rubbed behind Belle's ear. "I haven't decided yet what I'm going to do, but I guarantee it'll make all my old revenges look like picnics in the park!"

Carole and Lisa exchanged a worried glance. Once Stevie got started on a revenge, there was little chance of stopping her, and here it was, just before Christmas!

"Don't forget that it's that 'Peace on Earth, goodwill toward men' time of year, Stevie," Carole reminded her.

78

"I have goodwill toward everybody," said Stevie. "Everybody except Veronica, that is."

"Why don't we tack up and go for our ride?" Lisa suggested. "Maybe getting out in the nice cold air will make us all feel better."

"Okay," Stevie agreed. "Meet you at the horseshoe."

A few minutes later they were ready to go.

"We're doing the creek trail, aren't we?" asked Carole as Starlight stamped his front foot in anticipation.

"Right." Lisa gave Prancer's neck a pat. "I want to see if Prancer's gotten any better at going over water. I'm hoping you were right, Carole. Maybe the other day she was just having a bad creek day."

"It's worth a try." Carole looked at Prancer. "Sometimes horses get silly for no good reason. Then they get better and behave normally."

"Let's go," Stevie said. "We won't have much time before Carole has to go help her dad."

They rode around to the back of the stable, then trotted up the hill. The sun was a pale yellow ball in the western sky, barely glimmering behind the low, gray clouds. The horses' breath came out in puffs of steam in the cold air, making them look like wild, rampaging chargers instead of the well-trained mounts they were.

Carole took a deep breath of the damp December air. "It might not be the greatest weather to ride in, but it sure feels good to be outside. It seems like lately I'm either in school or helping my dad in that warehouse."

"How's the toy campaign coming?" Lisa asked.

"Wonderful," Carole replied. "Dad and I have sorted about a thousand toys, and more stuff comes in every day. The Marines have done a terrific job. I bet every needy child in Willow Creek will have some toys from that warehouse." Carole smiled as they rode along. It made her feel good to be doing something with her dad, but it made her feel even better to be helping people who weren't as lucky as she was.

"I'm really looking forward to helping you guys out." Lisa ducked as Prancer trotted under a low-hanging limb.

"We'll probably need you two in about a week," said Carole. "That's when the really fun part will start—delivering the toys to people."

"Hey, what do you guys think of this?" called Stevie, who was riding behind the other two. "What if I greased Veronica's new saddle right before the next mounted Horse Wise meeting? All she would be able to do then would be fall off."

Lisa frowned. "Well, Stevie, I think it would be really funny, but I think Veronica could get hurt and that would get you into a whole lot of trouble. Veronica's father would probably have you arrested and put in jail. And who knows what Max would do?"

"I don't think Max would even notice," said Stevie, urging Belle forward a little. "He's too busy running the stable and helping Deborah with Maxi to notice much of anything these days."

80

"You know, he and Deborah really have been busy lately," agreed Carole. "You never see them together just sitting down relaxing and having a good time."

"I guess that's part of having two jobs and a baby," Lisa said.

"And two dozen horses and a chapter of the Pony Club and about a zillion riding lessons every week," added Stevie.

"Well, yeah." Carole laughed. "I guess that would tire you out a little." She looked over her shoulder and grinned at Stevie. "I was amazed at the last Horse Wise. Max was even too tired to get mad at us when we sneaked in late."

"We just got lucky," said Stevie. "I thought he'd have me mucking out stalls for a week."

"Good thing for you guys he was thinking about Secret Santas," Lisa said with a laugh.

"Oh, please," Stevie groaned. "Don't remind me about Secret Santas. My Secret Santa situation has taken a definite turn for the worse."

"How about you, Lisa?" Carole asked. "Have you done your Secret Santa good deed?"

"I've been too busy cleaning and baking at home," replied Lisa. "Plus, I don't have any idea what to do."

"Me neither," said Carole. She looked at Lisa riding ahead of her and frowned. "This Secret Santa stuff is harder than it seems."

The girls crested the hill and began to follow the creek

81

that crisscrossed Pine Hollow's property and ultimately flowed through the town. The trail was well worn at the low places where horses had crossed the creek, and the usually soft ground had frozen hard and crusty.

"Well, here goes nothing," Lisa called as Prancer approached the first crossing.

"Try keeping her at an even trot and she might go on over before she knows she's done it," said Carole.

"And don't tense up yourself," Stevie reminded Lisa. "She'll feel your fear and get scared herself."

"That's a lot to remember," called Lisa. "But I'll try." She maintained her posting trot, took a deep breath, and relaxed her hands a bit. Prancer's ears flicked straight ahead as she trotted toward the creek. The water was coming closer and closer. *Oh, good,* thought Lisa as they neared the bank. *She's going over.*

But suddenly Prancer bobbed her head. She gave a little jump as if she might rear, took two steps sideways, then came to a dead stop.

"Give her some leg," called Carole. "Keep her moving!"

Lisa dug her heels into Prancer behind her girth. It did no good. Prancer just stood in the middle of the trail, still as a statue.

Carole and Stevie trotted up. "Let's go on over," said Stevie. "Her herd instinct might kick in and she might follow."

"Be my guest," said Lisa helplessly.

82

Stevie and Belle trotted across the wide, shallow creek, splashing as they went. Carole and Starlight followed. Both horses seemed to enjoy the cold water that bubbled around their feet. Prancer watched them cross with great interest, but she did not move from her spot.

"So much for awakening her herd instinct," said Lisa as Stevie and Carole turned and saw her still on the other side.

"Walk her in a circle and try again," suggested Carole. "Maybe when she sees us over here she'll cross."

"Okay." Lisa backed Prancer up, circled once, and approached the creek at a walk. She tried to remember to keep her hands loose and urge Prancer forward at the same time. Prancer walked forward willingly until she came to the creek. Though she saw Belle and Starlight waiting on the other side, she planted all four feet on the ground and refused to budge a step further.

Lisa looked sadly at her friends across the creek. "Any other ideas?"

"We could get off and push," suggested Stevie.

Carole laughed. "Gosh, Stevie. Prancer only outweighs all three of us by about a thousand pounds," she said. "I don't think we'd be able to push her anywhere."

"Well, we're going nowhere fast like this." Lisa sighed and dismounted. "I guess I'll have to lead her across like before."

She pulled the reins over Prancer's head and stepped to the edge of the creek. "Come on, girl," she murmured, giving the reins a gentle tug. Prancer stretched her neck out but did not move her feet.

Lisa stepped into the creek and splashed the water around her feet. "See, Prancer? It's just cold water. You drink gallons of it every day." Prancer blinked at the water.

Lisa waded out into the creek, where the water flowed over the tops of her feet. "Come on, Prancer," she said, lowering her voice to make it sound firm and commanding. "It's time to cross the creek!" With that she gave a sharp tug on the reins. Prancer did not budge, but suddenly Lisa's feet slid out from under her on the slick rocks in the creek. With a huge splash, she plopped down flat in the cold water.

"*Yeeeoooowwww!*" she cried. "This is freezing!" She scrambled to her feet, still holding Prancer's reins. She was dripping wet from the waist down.

"Lisa, are you okay?" called Carole.

"I think so," said Lisa as she clambered back to Prancer. "I'm just cold. No wonder Prancer doesn't want to cross that creek. The water is like ice!"

Stevie and Carole recrossed the creek and pulled up beside Lisa and Prancer. Lisa's face was bright red. Her pants and boots were soaked.

"Are you sure you're okay?" Stevie frowned at Lisa's soggy breeches.

"Just slightly humiliated," Lisa replied. "Not only can I

not get my horse to cross the creek, but apparently I can't even get myself across the creek." She looked at Prancer and began to laugh. "We're going to make a fine team at the Fairfax trail ride, Prancer. They'll have to build special little barges and ferry us across the streams!"

Carole and Stevie joined in Lisa's laughter. Though they were relieved that she wasn't hurt, they were equally relieved that she was laughing. They knew what a perfectionist she could be, and sometimes her determination to succeed could take over her life.

"Well, what now?" asked Lisa, wiping tears of laughter from her eyes.

"We'd better get you back to the stable," said Stevie. "You might get hypothermia."

"Stevie, we're only ten minutes away from the stable." Lisa eyed the creek again. "If I don't get Prancer crossing creeks again soon, I'm going to have to forget about Fairfax. This may be my last chance to work with her before all my relatives come over from Scotland. They'll be here in just a couple of days, and my mother hasn't baked half of what she's got planned!"

"Well, I'm going to have to go help my dad pretty soon, and since you're soaking wet, maybe we ought to go back to Pine Hollow," said Carole. "I don't think there's much we can do about Prancer this afternoon."

"Okay," Lisa agreed reluctantly. "I guess you're right." She climbed back up on Prancer, creek water dripping from her breeches. "Ugh." She shivered. "This feels wet and cold and really gross. A nice warm stable is sounding better and better."

Prancer turned around and began trotting briskly after Stevie and Belle. Carole and Starlight fell in behind. Carole laughed as she listened to the squishing sound Lisa made every time she posted. Though Lisa was soaking wet and Stevie was raging mad, suddenly Carole was very happy. She had just figured out exactly what her Secret Santa gift was going to be!

IT WAS ALMOST dusk by the time the girls got back to Pine
Hollow. Deborah and Mrs. Reg were gone, but Max was
still giving adult dressage lessons.

"Gosh, it's still busy here," Lisa said as they walked
their horses toward their stalls. Just as they turned the
corner, a familiar voice rang out.

"Hi, girls. How's it going?"

They turned. Colonel Hanson stood by Starlight's
stall.

"Hi, Colonel Hanson," Stevie and Lisa said together.

"Hi, Dad." Carole handed Lisa Starlight's reins and ran
to give her father a hug. "How come you're here?"

"I knocked off early at work and came by to see if you

87

were here." He grinned. "The moment I saw Starlight's empty stall I knew I was right."

"We took a trail ride along the creek," Carole explained as her father held open Starlight's door.

"Looks like somebody took a trail ride *in* the creek." Colonel Hanson eyed Lisa's drenched breeches.

"Actually, I didn't fall in," explained Lisa, her cheeks growing pink. "I was trying to get Prancer to cross the creek and I slipped on some rocks and—"

"Say no more," Colonel Hanson said with a smile. "I understand completely. All in the line of duty."

"Hey, Colonel Hanson," Stevie called as she removed Belle's saddle. "I've got a Christmas joke for you."

"I was hoping you might, Stevie." Colonel Hanson and Stevie shared a love of old jokes—the cornier the better.

Stevie leaned over the stall door and grinned. "If athletes get athlete's foot, what do astronauts get?"

Colonel Hanson frowned a moment. "I don't know. What?"

"Missile toe!"

"Oh, no," Carole and Lisa groaned while Colonel Hanson and Stevie laughed.

"That's pretty good, Stevie," Colonel Hanson said, chuckling. "I'll have to come up with one for you next time." He watched as the girls put their horses into their stalls. "I actually came here for a reason. I was going to

88

take Carole over to do our shift at the toy warehouse and I wondered if you two would like to come along. We can grab some burgers and fries on the way, and I'll have you home by nine."

"Thanks, Colonel Hanson, but I'd better not." Lisa sighed. "We've got company coming for Christmas and I've got to help my mom get ready."

"I can't, either," said Stevie. "I'd love to, but I've got a big algebra test tomorrow, and if I don't study hard tonight I'm sure I'll get an F."

"I understand," said Colonel Hanson. "Duty comes first. We'll have some fun distributing the toys later."

"Right." Stevie grinned. "We're really looking forward to that!"

A little while later, as the horses were munching their evening hay, Colonel Hanson gave Lisa and Stevie a ride home. Then he and Carole turned toward the toy warehouse.

"Okay," Colonel Hanson said. "Last time it was a Hanson special. How about a Nick's double burger combo tonight?"

"Sounds great," replied Carole. "I'm starved."

They drove to Nick's Drive In and ordered double burgers, fries, and two chocolate shakes. Then they headed across town. Colonel Hanson tuned the radio to his favorite oldies station, and they ate as they drove through the cold December night. One of the things Carole loved the most about her dad was that he liked doing things most parents didn't like to do—like eating burgers in the car while listening to fifties rock and roll.

Colonel Hanson took the downtown route to get to the warehouse. They passed lots of stores and businesses that were brightly decorated with twinkling Christmas lights.

"Christmas is so pretty." Carole sipped her milk shake as she gazed out the window. "If only it would snow."

"Well, there's still time," her father said, smiling. "You never know what kind of weather system might blow down from Canada in the next week."

They drove through the business district and on into the warehouse area. Down here no decorations adorned the buildings, and few had lights of any kind.

"I like the warehouse, Dad, but this section of town gives me the creeps." Carole shivered in spite of her warm parka.

"I know what you mean." Colonel Hanson again locked the car doors. "It is pretty seedy."

After twisting through several streets, they finally reached the warehouse. It looked darker and more run-down than ever, sitting in the middle of the deserted parking lot.

"It's funny how so many bright, happy things are inside this gloomy-looking building, isn't it?" Carole said as they got out of the car.

"I know." Her father fumbled for the warehouse keys. "It's like going from night to day."

He found the right key, and they walked to the door. In the darkness it was hard to see. Colonel Hanson leaned down over the heavy chain that held the door shut and looked for the lock.

"Hmmm," he muttered when he found it. "Captain Barnard didn't secure this lock completely last night. That's not what I call running a tight ship."

He pulled the lock and chain aside, then pushed the door open. Inside, the warehouse was dark and cold. "Now, where is that light switch?" he said as Carole followed close behind him.

"I think it's over to the right," she said.

"Okay." He felt along the wall for a moment, then found it. A loud click echoed as he turned the switch on. Carole blinked, expecting the bright colors of a thousand piled-up toys to explode before her eyes, but instead, there was nothing. All she saw was space. The warehouse was empty!

"What happened?" she gasped as she looked at the vacant grayness. "Where are all the toys? Did somebody move them?"

"Nobody in my command did," said Colonel Hanson, his voice tight. Slowly he turned around, as if he couldn't believe his eyes. There wasn't a single toy left in the building.

"Quick, honey!" He put his arm around Carole. "Let's get out of here!"

They hurried back to their car. Colonel Hanson locked the doors and punched in 911 on his car phone.

"This is Colonel Mitch Hanson, United States Marine Corps," he said when the police dispatcher answered. "I'm calling to report a robbery at eighty-seven Wharf Avenue. It's the Marine Corps toy drive warehouse. We've been cleaned out."

Colonel Hanson answered a few more questions, then put the phone down.

"Are the police coming?" Carole asked, her heart thudding in her chest. She'd never been involved in a crime before.

"They're on their way. The dispatcher said if we weren't in any danger to remain on the scene. They'd like to get a statement from us."

"Dad?" asked Carole in a small voice. "Are we in any danger?"

"I don't think so, honey." Her dad shook his head. "I think whoever stole these toys is long gone."

They stayed in their car, thinking about all the toys that were gone. In a few minutes two police cars came roaring up, their lights flashing and sirens yowling. Colonel Hanson got out of the car and led the officers to the building. A few moments later a red station wagon pulled into the parking lot. Carole caught her breath in astonishment as Deborah, Max's wife, got out of the front seat, a pencil and pad in her hand.

"Deborah!" Carole rolled down her window. "What are you doing here?"

Deborah blinked with surprise when she saw Carole. "I'm covering the police beat for another reporter who's having a baby. We heard about this on our scanner. What are you doing here?"

"My dad's in charge of the toy drive this year," explained Carole. "We had just come down here to work when we found everything gone."

"Well, of course. I should have remembered your dad was a Marine." Deborah gave Carole a quick smile, then turned toward the warehouse. "Right now, though, I need to go find out what's going on!"

A photographer got out of the station wagon and followed Deborah. Colonel Hanson and the police were just going inside the building. "Wait for me," Carole said as she scrambled out of her car and hurried to join everyone else.

Inside, the police officers had begun to investigate the warehouse. One was examining the lock, which Colonel Hanson had removed from the chain; two others were shining flashlights along the floor, looking for footprints; the fourth was talking to Carole's dad. Deborah was making notes on her pad while the photographer shot pictures of the police examining the huge empty space. Carole walked over and stood close beside her father.

"You say everything was in order here last night?" the police officer asked.

"Yes, Sergeant Lewandowski. Everything was fine last night when Captain Barnard finished his detail here and locked up."

"And what time was that?" Sergeant Lewandowski scribbled on a pad much like Deborah's.

"I believe he left here last night about eleven."

"Okay." The sergeant looked at what he had written. "Let me go check and see what the others have come up with."

Carole watched as the officers huddled in the center of the empty warehouse. Deborah stepped forward and spoke to her father.

"Hi, Mitch," Deborah said.

"Hi, Deborah. What are you doing here?" Carole's father said, smiling a little.

"I'm covering this story tonight for a friend. Can you tell me a little more about what happened?"

Colonel Hanson began to tell Deborah about how hard the Marines had worked all year, and how they had hoped that this year every needy child in Willow Creek and the rest of the county would get a toy. Deborah scribbled on her pad as he spoke and had just begun to ask him another question when Sergeant Lewandowski interrupted.

"I hate to have to tell you this, Colonel, but it looks

like there's not going to be a lot we can do. Whoever did this has done it before. There's nothing we can get a clue off of—all the fingerprints have been wiped clean, there are no footprints, and there aren't any marks on the lock to indicate that a special tool was used to open it. There might be tire tracks, but the ground is frozen, so we won't find much there."

Sergeant Lewandowski pushed his police cap back on his head. "I'm awfully sorry. I wish I could guarantee that we could go out and catch these thieves, but it looks like a lot of little kids are going to be disappointed this Christmas."

"Are you sure there's nothing you can do?" Colonel Hanson asked with a frown.

"We'll do everything we can, sir," Sergeant Lewandowski replied. "We'll enter it in the crime computer and keep you posted should we get any leads. Unfortunately, a lot of expert thieves run loose at Christmastime."

"Well, thank you for coming." The two men shook hands while the other three police officers walked back to the patrol cars. Colonel Hanson looked around the empty warehouse and gave a big sigh.

"All that work," he said, smiling at Carole sadly.

"What are the Marines going to do now, Mitch?" Deborah asked. "Forget about this Christmas and concentrate on next year?"

Colonel Hanson looked at Deborah for a moment, then straightened his shoulders. "No, we're not going to forget about this year. The United States Marine Corps will deliver toys as planned. We're just going to have to work harder and faster to do it. From here on out, we'll be playing catch-up ball."

"May I quote you on that?" Deborah asked as she wrote frantically in her notebook.

"Yes, you may. The Marines will accomplish this mission, whatever it takes."

A twinkle suddenly came into Deborah's eyes. "Well, Mitch, maybe the paper can help you out some. Hey, John," she called to her photographer. "Come get a shot of Colonel Hanson and Carole. I bet the city editor will put this on the front page for human interest."

"Really?" said Carole. She couldn't imagine having her picture on the front page of the paper.

"I bet he will," said Deborah with a grin. "And I know somebody else who might be able to help you out, too. Just a minute."

She stepped to one side while the photographer was taking their picture and punched in a number on her cell phone. She spoke softly into the phone for a moment, then snapped it shut.

"Okay," she said, returning to Carole and her dad. "Do you guys know who Tress Montgomery is?"

"Sure," replied Carole, thinking of the glamorous TV reporter who was on the news every night. "Everybody knows who Tress Montgomery is."

"Well, she's on her way over here right now. I told her

what a jam you guys were in and she wants to do a report for the eleven o'clock news. They were just wrapping up a story from the mayor's office, so they should be here in about five minutes."

Carole's jaw dropped. Not only were they going to be in the paper, they were going to be on TV as well! This was the most unbelievable night she'd ever spent. First a robbery, then a newspaper reporter, now a TV crew!

"That's awfully nice of you, Deborah." Colonel Hanson smiled. "I don't know how to thank you."

"I figure helping you out with a little publicity is the least I can do." Deborah smiled at Carole. "I'd hate to think of some little child not getting anything for Christmas. Even little Maxi gets excited when she sees packages wrapped up, and she's just a baby."

A few minutes later they heard a loud knock on the warehouse door.

"Hello?" a familiar voice called. "Anybody here?"

"Hi, Tress," Deborah answered. "Come on in. Everybody's in here."

Carole couldn't believe her eyes. Into the empty warehouse walked Tress Montgomery with a video cameraman behind her. She looked just as glamorous as she did on television—beautiful clothes, curly black hair, big brown eyes, and a gorgeous smile. "Hi, Deborah," she said in her famous husky voice. "How are you?"

"I'm fine, Tress," Deborah replied. "But we've got a

Marine colonel and his daughter here who could use a little assistance."

Tress Montgomery walked over to them. "Tress, this is Colonel Mitch Hanson and his daughter, Carole," Deborah said.

"Hi." Tress smiled warmly at both Carole and her dad. "Deborah tells me you've had some trouble here."

"We have," Colonel Hanson began. He told Tress the whole story. She, like Deborah, took notes on a pad. Then she turned to her cameraman.

"Scooter, get some exterior footage on the building, then come inside and I'll interview Colonel Hanson and Carole."

The cameraman lifted the heavy camera to his shoulder and walked outside to shoot the building. "Okay," said Tress. "When he comes back inside, I'll ask you two some questions. You just look in the camera as you answer, and everything will be fine. Okay?"

Colonel Hanson nodded. Carole began to get butterflies in her stomach. What would she say if Tress Montgomery asked her any questions? A few minutes later the cameraman came back. He had attached a special light bar to his camera that lit up a small area of the warehouse as bright as day. Carole blinked as Tress Montgomery stood in front of the camera and began to speak.

"I'm standing here in a warehouse that just yesterday held thousands of toys, all ready to be delivered to the needy children of this county. . . . ," she said into a microphone. She reported on the theft of the toys, then turned to Carole and her dad.

"Here with me now is Colonel Mitch Hanson, the Marine Corps officer in charge of this year's annual Christmas toy drive. Colonel Hanson, I know you and your daughter, Carole, have volunteered many long hours on this project. How does it feel to come in here and find all your work gone?"

"I'm disgusted and amazed that anybody would stoop to stealing toys from poor children," Colonel Hanson said, his voice stern.

"And Carole? How does this make you feel?" Tress Montgomery pointed the microphone at Carole.

"I'm sad that it happened." Carole's mouth felt dry and full of cotton. She hoped her voice wasn't coming out all quivery. "A lot of little kids are going to be disappointed."

Tress Montgomery returned to her father. "What's the plan now, Colonel Hanson? With Christmas just days away, is the Corps going to scrub this operation and concentrate on next Christmas?"

"No, ma'am," Colonel Hanson said emphatically. "The United States Marine Corps will deliver toys to needy children this Christmas, as scheduled. I'm not quite sure how we're going to do it, but we'll work twice as hard and twice as fast to make sure it gets done."

Tress smiled and pushed the microphone back into Carole's face. "And how about you, Carole? Are you willing to work twice as hard and twice as fast as before?"

"Oh, yes," said Carole. "I'll help my dad do whatever needs to be done. I know my friends will help, too."

Tress turned back to the camera. "So that's the story from eighty-seven Wharf Avenue, folks. Though all the toys have been stolen, Colonel Mitch Hanson and his daughter, Carole, vow that they'll do whatever it takes to make sure no needy child goes without Christmas this year. This is Tress Montgomery reporting for Channel Four News."

Tress stopped talking and looked expectantly at the cameraman. He checked his camera and nodded. "Got it," he said as he switched off the bright lights. "It's a wrap!"

Tress Montgomery turned back to Carole and her dad. "Thank you so much. This will go on the air tonight at eleven, and maybe tomorrow evening as well. I hope that will help get the Marines' toy campaign going again."

"Thanks, Ms. Montgomery." Colonel Hanson extended his hand, and she clasped it. "We appreciate any and all publicity."

Tress Montgomery looked at the empty space and shook her head. "Personally, I think it's going to be tough to fill this warehouse again so close to Christmas, but if anybody can do it, the Marines can." She smiled at Carole and her dad as she turned to go. "Good luck," she said. "I hope this report helps."

"Thanks again." Colonel Hanson and Carole watched

as Tress Montgomery and her photographer walked back to their van. Then they were alone.

"Gosh, Dad, do you think we can really replace all these toys?" Carole asked softly.

"I don't know, honey," Colonel Hanson replied. "It's going to take an enormous amount of work, but we're sure going to give it our best shot."

"Well, The Saddle Club will do everything we can to help," Carole said, volunteering Lisa and Stevie. She knew they would help regardless of whatever else was on their busy schedules. After all, helping each other was what The Saddle Club was all about. "We'll start tomorrow, right after school."

"That's my girl." Colonel Hanson smiled at her proudly and held out his hand for a high five. *"Semper Fi!"*

11

"CAROLE!" STEVIE RAN into the tack room. Riding class was about to start and she was running late, as usual. Most of the other riders were already warming up their horses.

Carole looked up from the bench where she was sitting, lacing up her field boots. "Stevie! Where have you been? I've been dying to talk to you!"

"I saw you on TV last night." The words tumbled out of Stevie's mouth as she sat down beside Carole. "You were in a robbery! And look." She held up the front section of the morning newspaper. "You're also in the paper! Are you okay? I wanted to call you last night but my mom wouldn't let me. She said if you'd been hurt you'd have been in the hospital and not on television, which"—Stevie gasped for breath—"makes sense, I suppose."

"I'm fine," Carole said. "It was the most unbelievable

night I've ever spent." She looked at Stevie and frowned. "How come you saw me on TV? I didn't come on until after eleven. Weren't you in bed?"

"No, I had to study for my algebra test. I was just brushing my teeth when my mom called me downstairs to see you on TV. You looked really good."

"Carole!" Both girls looked up. Lisa stood there, the front page of the paper also in her hand. "Look! You're in the paper!"

"I know," Carole said calmly. Though it was exciting to be in the paper, her friends at school had asked her the same questions all day long, and she had been giving the same answers since early morning.

Lisa frowned. "But it said you were in a robbery. Are you all right? How's your dad?"

"Oh, I'm fine, thanks," Carole replied. "And so is Dad. The worst part is that the toys are all gone."

"All of them?" Stevie blinked in disbelief as she began to pull on the battered cowboy boots she rode in.

"Every one of them." Carole's voice was sad. "The warehouse is totally empty."

"Wow," said Lisa. "You were at a real crime scene."

"Is it just like on television?" Stevie asked. "Did the cops come roaring up with their guns drawn, barking orders over a bullhorn?"

Carole shook her head. "They drove up with their sirens on, but after that it was pretty dull. They just looked for clues and asked my dad a lot of questions."

"Like 'Where were you on the night of December ninth?' " Stevie asked in a deep voice.

"No." Carole had to laugh at Stevie's imitation of a police officer. "More like 'Colonel Hanson, when were all the toys last accounted for?' "

"Gosh, Carole, weren't you scared?" Lisa sat down next to her.

Carole nodded. "I was when we first went inside. We turned on the lights, expecting to see all these toys, and there was nothing there. It gave me a really creepy feeling. I was afraid the thieves might still be around the building, hiding and waiting for us."

"What did you do?" asked Stevie.

"We ran back out to our car. My dad locked the doors and called 911 on his car phone. He sounded so serious that I got even more scared. Then the police came. And then Deborah pulled up right after the police."

"Our Deborah?" Stevie's eyebrows lifted in surprise.

Carole nodded. "She was covering the police beat for another reporter. She's the one who got our picture in the paper and asked Tress Montgomery to come and interview us."

"Wow," said Lisa dreamily as she retrieved her riding helmet. "You actually met *the* Tress Montgomery. Is she as glamorous in person as she is on television?"

"She is." Carole remembered Tress's beautiful clothes and friendly smile. "She's really nice, too. She said she hoped that putting us on television would get people interested in helping the Marines replace the stolen toys."

"Gosh, that's a lot of toys to replace and not a lot of time." Stevie threw her sneakers into her cubby. "Does your dad think they can do it?"

"They're going to try," Carole replied proudly. "He said the Marine Corps would accomplish their mission." She looked at both her friends. "I told him The Saddle Club would help."

"Of course we will," said Lisa. "But how?"

"I don't know." Carole frowned. "I haven't gotten that far. But I know we can do most anything once we put our minds to it. Think of all the other things we've accomplished together. Raising a few thousand toys in the next few days shouldn't be too hard."

"That's right," said Stevie. "We've just got to think of this as a challenge. Problems aren't really problems, they're just opportunities to learn." She wrapped a red plaid scarf around her neck. "Why, just this afternoon I thought of a wonderful new trick to play on Veronica. You know how she comes in here and—"

Lisa cleared her throat loudly. Stevie looked up. Veronica had walked into the room and stopped in front of her locker, which was just across the aisle from Stevie's cubby. Veronica insisted on having a locker with a door to protect her valuable riding gear—from Stevie's pranks more than anything else.

"Hi," she said. She caught a glimpse of the newspaper in Lisa's hand and smirked at Carole. "I saw your picture in the paper this morning. Of course it wasn't on the society page where it really counts, but it was an okay picture."

"Thanks, Veronica," replied Carole.

"Anyway, my father said we need to be generous to people who are less fortunate, particularly at Christmastime, so here's a contribution for the toy drive." Veronica dug in her expensive leather purse and pulled out a dollar. "Here." She held the crisp bill out to Carole.

"Thanks, Veronica." Carole took the money. "I'll give it to my dad."

"Please do," Veronica said. "And tell him it's from the diAngelo family."

"I'm sure the Marines will be overwhelmed, Veronica," Stevie said sarcastically. "They might even give you a medal."

Veronica tossed her head, swinging her smooth black hair in Stevie's direction, then turned to her locker. She started to open it, then stopped. She turned back to Stevie. "You haven't been doing anything to my locker, have you?" she asked, her green eyes narrowing.

"No," Stevie replied with a clear conscience. "I've been sitting here talking to Carole and Lisa."

"Are you sure?" Veronica's voice was tinged with suspicion.

"Positive." Stevie zipped up her old quilted riding jacket. "I'm just getting ready to ride."

"Hmmmm." Veronica turned back to her locker while Stevie grinned at Lisa and Carole. They sat back on the bench and watched. Veronica slowly began to open her locker an inch at a time, as if she expected a rubber snake to come bursting out. Everyone held their breath as the door opened wider and wider. Carole and Lisa looked at each other. Had Stevie's awful revenge already begun?

Finally Veronica opened the door all the way. Lisa and Carole peered inside. Everything in the locker seemed normal, or at least normal for Veronica. Tall black leather boots stood gleaming on the floor; her elegant custom-tailored riding jacket hung above them; a box of fancy Italian chocolates sat on the top shelf.

"What did you expect to find in there, Veronica?" Stevie asked innocently. "A dead body?"

"No, of course not," Veronica replied haughtily, though she carefully peeked into the dark corners of the locker before she hung up her parka. Stevie, Carole, and Lisa tried hard not to laugh as she turned each boot upside down and shook it before she pulled it onto her foot. Then she checked the pockets of her jacket to make sure nothing disgusting had been hidden there.

"Well," she said airily, trying to disguise the nervousness in her voice. "Everything seems fine. See you in class."

"Have a good lesson," Stevie called. "And don't forget to check your stirrup leathers. You never know what can happen around here at Christmastime!"

Veronica gave Stevie a nervous glance over her shoulder and hurried out to Danny's stall.

Carole and Lisa burst out laughing as soon as Veronica had left the tack room. "Stevie, what did you do to her stirrup leathers?" Carole asked.

"Nothing," said Stevie, her hazel eyes twinkling with delight. "I haven't done anything to her at all. I've thought about doing a lot of stuff to her, but I haven't had time to put any of my plans into action."

"But she thinks you've booby-trapped everything!" Lisa said.

"I know," Stevie said, bursting into giggles herself. "That's what's so wonderful. I haven't done a thing. It's Veronica's guilty conscience that's making her think I have." Stevie grinned. "This is great. This is better than anything I could ever have dreamed up. All I have to do is sit back and be nice to Veronica. It'll drive her crazy!"

"Stevie, that's psychological warfare!" Carole laughed.

"I know." Stevie grinned. "I'm getting my revenge and I'm not doing a thing! I might start being even nicer to her. That will really drive her nuts!"

"Okay, girls, get a move on! You've got ten minutes to tack up and get ready for class!" Max breezed by the door carrying some orange plastic cones. A second later he came back and stood in the doorway.

"Carole, are you okay? Deborah said you and your dad had some trouble last night." Max's blue eyes clouded with concern.

Carole nodded. "I'm fine, Max. The toy drive is ruined, though."

"That's too bad," Max said. "Maybe all your publicity will help get things going again." He started back to the riding ring, then paused and gave Stevie a hard look. "Ten minutes! And no excuses for being late today!"

"Let's go," said Lisa. "He's not kidding."

"But what are we going to do to help the Marines?" asked Carole as they hurried down to their horses' stalls. "We had just begun to talk about it when Veronica came in."

"Let's have a Saddle Club meeting at TD's after class," suggested Stevie. "That way maybe we can all three come up with some good ways to raise money."

"I don't know if I can come," said Lisa with a frown. "I'm supposed to go home and help my mother bake five dozen bannocks. Our relatives are scheduled to arrive from Scotland tomorrow afternoon." She looked at Stevie and Carole and sighed. "But I think this qualifies as a Saddle Club emergency. Mother and her bannocks will just have to wait."

"Great!" said Stevie. "We can get an ice cream and figure out what to do."

"Right now we'd better get our horses saddled," said Carole as they rushed toward the stalls. "Otherwise Max will figure out some nice barn chores for us."

12

LATER THAT AFTERNOON, after Prancer, Starlight, and Belle had been put back into their stalls and been given an armful of hay for the night, Stevie, Carole, and Lisa crossed the street in front of TD's.

"I can't believe how early it gets dark in December," Lisa said as they cautiously crossed in front of a bus with its headlights already on.

"I know," said Carole with a shiver. "And so cold."

"That means it's just the right time for ice cream." Stevie held TD's door open. "It gets you so cold on the inside, when you go back outside you don't feel it anymore."

"Huh?" said Lisa, frowning.

"Don't ask." Carole shook her head. "It's Stevian logic. Mere mortals can't understand."

111

They slid into their favorite booth. "What are you going to have this afternoon, Stevie?" Lisa asked. "Something new?"

Stevie wrinkled her brow in thought. "I might make up the Veronica special," she said. "That would be licorice ice cream with bittersweet chocolate sauce and devil's-food sprinkles." Stevie stuck out her tongue. "All dark and nasty and bitter."

Carole laughed. "You may be on to something with your psychological warfare, Stevie. Did you see how Veronica acted during riding class?"

"I know," said Lisa. "Most of the time she kept checking her stirrup leathers. And when she wasn't doing that she kept looking around the ring to see where you and Belle were."

Stevie made her eyes bug out. "You never know what can happen when your mind starts playing tricks on you."

Their usual waitress came over to the table, order pad in hand. "What'll it be today, girls?" she asked. Then she looked at Carole. "Say, wasn't that you in the paper this morning? And on TV last night? With the stolen toys?"

Carole smiled. "Yes, that was me."

"Your dad's the Marine in charge of that toy drive. That's really awful, that somebody would steal toys that were meant for poor kids."

"Yes, it is," Carole agreed. "We're trying to come up with ways to help right now."

"Well, good for you," said the waitress. "That's a real

nice thing to do." She pulled her pencil from behind her ear. "What can I get for you this afternoon?"

"I think I'll have hot chocolate," said Carole, unbuttoning her jacket. "With extra marshmallows."

"Me too," Lisa chimed in. "It's just too cold for ice cream."

"Not for me," said Stevie. "I'd like my Christmas special, please."

The waitress frowned. "Your Christmas special? Refresh my memory—was that the raspberry sherbet with the marshmallow sauce or the French vanilla with the chopped green cherries?"

"Actually it was one scoop of pistachio with strawberry sauce and coconut sprinkles." Stevie smiled. "You were close, though."

The waitress shook her head, scribbled their orders on her pad, and walked back to the counter.

"Gosh, Carole," Stevie said in a low voice. "You're a regular celebrity."

"Yeah," agreed Lisa. "I'm surprised she didn't ask you for your autograph."

"Okay, okay," said Carole with an embarrassed smile. "Right now I call this meeting of The Saddle Club to order. We've got to hurry and think of a way to help the Marines raise a couple of thousand toys."

The girls were silent for a moment. Then Lisa spoke. "I wonder if there's anything we could sell," she said. "People are always needing stuff to buy at Christmastime."

113

"We could have a trash and treasure sale." Stevie untied the red scarf from her neck. "There's lots of stuff in my closet we could sell."

"Stevie, we'd have to pay someone to haul the junk in your closet away," said Carole with a laugh. "I've seen what's in there, and I don't think anybody would be interested in buying it."

"I guess you're right," Stevie said with a sigh. "I probably do have a lot more trash than treasure."

The girls gazed at the empty table before them, trying to come up with an idea. "How about a bake sale?" Carole finally suggested. "We could bake cookies and cupcakes at home and sell them to hungry shoppers at the mall."

"That wouldn't work for me," said Lisa glumly. "I'm too busy baking scones and shortbread and bannocks for my mom to bake anything extra."

"Me neither." Stevie looked embarrassed. "I'm not such a hot baker to begin with. The last cookies I baked came out of the oven as hard as rocks. Alex and Chad actually used them as hockey pucks at the ice rink one afternoon."

The waitress returned and put two cups of hot chocolate with extra marshmallows in front of them, along with Stevie's red, white, and green sundae. "Enjoy," she said, shaking her head at Stevie as she walked back to the counter.

"There must be something we can do." Carole frowned as she wrapped her hands around her cup.

"I've got it!" cried Lisa. "This is so easy! Why don't we set up a booth and just collect contributions? People shopping could come by and drop either money or toys right in. We could use a big cardboard box and paint a sign over it saying what we're doing. We could work every afternoon after school and all day Saturday."

"That's a great idea!" said Stevie. "We wouldn't have to bake anything or haul a bunch of junk out of our closets."

"And we could work in shifts, so all of us wouldn't have to be there all the time," added Carole. "You're a genius, Lisa!"

"Thanks," Lisa said with a smile.

"Where could we set the booth up?" asked Stevie as she took a big bite of ice cream.

"Why not right here, in front of TD's?" said Lisa. "They probably wouldn't mind, and Stevie can run in for refreshments if she starts feeling faint."

"Good thinking," said Stevie. "But we'll have to ask the manager."

"Maybe the waitress will ask him for us," said Lisa. "Carole, you ask her. She thinks you're a celebrity."

"You really think so?" Carole took a sip of her hot chocolate.

Stevie nodded. "Absolutely. You've got the best chance

with her. She thinks I'm crazy, and she doesn't really know Lisa, but you—you're a big star."

Just then the waitress came over to the table with their checks. "Anything else I can get you girls?"

"Actually, there is." Carole took a deep breath. "We're trying to raise money to help out my dad and the Marine Corps, and we were wondering if we might set up a collection booth outside your store."

"A collection booth?" The waitress frowned.

"Yes. We'd like to collect money and toys from the people who shop at this center. We'd have a sign, and we'd stay away from your door and everything. And we'd be gone by Christmas Eve."

The waitress gave a quizzical frown. "If it were up to me, I'd say sure, but I'll have to ask the manager. Sit right there and let me see what he says."

She went behind the counter and disappeared into the back room. For a long moment nothing happened.

"What do you think he's saying?" Stevie asked in a whisper. "Maybe he thinks we're just too weird and he doesn't want us hanging around the shop at all."

"Oh, Stevie, don't be paranoid," said Lisa. "We're good customers. We may be a little weird, but think of all the hundreds of dollars we've spent on ice cream in the past year."

In a moment the waitress appeared from the back room and walked over to their table. "The manager says okay.

116

Normally he wouldn't go for it, but I told him you were good kids and this was for a real good cause. And, shoot, it's Christmas, isn't it?"

"Thanks," the girls all said together.

"We really appreciate it," Carole added with a smile.

"I hope you get lots of money," the waitress said as she took the money for their ice cream. "Imagine, people mean enough to steal toys from needy children." She shook her head again as she walked to the cash register.

"Okay," Carole said, leaning over the table excitedly. "So far, so good. Now what?"

"My parents just got a new TV set," said Stevie. "The box is huge and it's still in the garage. We could use that."

"I could work the first shift tomorrow after school," Lisa volunteered. "My Scottish relatives are due in late tomorrow afternoon, but I could work until they come."

"Okay," said Carole. "Then I'll make the sign. I think we've got some cardboard at home I can use."

"All right," Stevie said. "Then, Carole, you make the sign, I'll bring the box, and we'll all meet here tomorrow as soon after school as we possibly can. We'll set up right outside the door, so everyone who walks down this way will be sure to see us. If they ask what we're doing, we'll say we're The Saddle Club from Pine Hollow Stables, and we're proud to be helping the U.S. Marines."

"Sounds good to me," said Carole with a grin.

Stevie held her hand up for a high five. "Then the Marines can relax! The Saddle Club is on the job! And with a few good girls to help them out, it's bound to be a success!"

13

THE NEXT AFTERNOON Carole and Lisa met in front of TD's. Though the air was cold, the sun was bright and the area was teeming with shoppers. Carole carried a large sign attached to a rake handle, while Lisa had brought a manila envelope to store their money in.

"Wonder where Stevie is?" Lisa asked, looking around the parking lot for the Lakes' station wagon.

"Her school gets out later than ours does," replied Carole. "She'll probably be here in a few minutes. Let's go ahead and lean our sign up against the building."

Lisa looked at the sign Carole had made. HELP THE U.S. MARINE CORPS CHRISTMAS TOY DRIVE was spelled out in bright red letters, but a curious, blobby-looking ball was splattered in the middle of the sign. Lisa frowned. "What's that basketball thing supposed to be?"

119

"The Marine Corps insignia." Carole gave a sheepish laugh and shrugged. "It doesn't look much like the world with an anchor through it, does it?"

Lisa tilted her head to one side and squinted with one eye. "Well, it kind of does if you look at it this way."

Carole giggled. "I guess I'm not such a great artist. Maybe people will just read the letters and not notice anything else."

Just then a woman carrying a shopping bag from an expensive store came out of TD's. She wore a long fur coat with a matching fur hat. Lisa nudged Carole with her elbow. "Look," she whispered with excitement. "Our first customer!" She stepped forward.

"Excuse me, ma'am, but we're collecting money to help the Marines replace the stolen toys." Lisa held open her envelope. "Would you like to make a donation?"

"Not today," the woman snapped. She gave Lisa and Carole a funny look and clutched her shopping bag close to her chest as she hurried down the sidewalk.

"Gosh." Carole blinked. "Wonder what was the matter with her?"

"I don't think we look professional." Lisa frowned. "I mean, it's just you standing there with a sign and me with an envelope. We need Stevie and that big box. It's almost three-thirty. Where could she be?"

Suddenly they heard a car horn. They looked across the parking lot. There, scrambling out of the back of the Lakes' station wagon, was Stevie, carrying a huge box

120

high above her head. It had pictures of toys pasted to it, and it was almost bigger than she was.

"Look!" Carole laughed. "She looks like a human box with legs!"

Stevie teetered across the street carrying the box, finally careening onto the sidewalk. "There!" she said with a gasp. "Here's the collection box. Sorry I'm late. We had to drop Alex off at basketball practice."

"It's okay," said Carole. "We've only had one customer, anyway."

"Did we get any money?" Stevie asked, her eyes bright.

Lisa shook her head. "No. I don't think the woman took us seriously. But everybody will now, since you brought that box. Those pictures on it look great."

"Thanks. My mom said we could bring out old beach chairs to sit in. They're in the back of the car." Stevie ran to her car and returned with three aluminum chairs. Carole arranged the box just beside TD's front window and leaned the sign up against the wall. Once they were set up, Mrs. Lake waved and drove off.

"There," said Stevie, stepping back to survey their collection booth. "It looks good. Now all we have to do is wait for people to come by. I bet we'll have a hundred dollars by the time my mom picks us up."

They unfolded their chairs, sat down behind the box, and waited. Several people in cars drove by and looked at their sign, while a few other shoppers went into the electronics store near TD's. One man stopped and said how terrible it was that criminals were now stealing from needy children. He wished them lots of luck but donated no money. A little later two other women stopped because they'd seen Carole on television.

"Is Tress Montgomery as glamorous in person as she is on the air?" asked a woman who wore bright purple earmuffs.

"Yes," answered Carole. "And she's very concerned about all the toys being stolen. Would you like to give a donation?"

"I'm on a real tight budget because of Christmas," the earmuffed lady explained. "But I can give a little," she added as she dropped a dollar into Stevie's box.

For a long time nobody else came by. The sun began to set and the air grew colder. Far down at the other end of the walkway the girls could see another person collecting for another charity, only this person was dressed in a Santa Claus suit and was ringing a bell.

"Maybe tomorrow we should bring a bell and dress up in Santa Claus suits," said Stevie with a sigh, eyeing the single dollar lying in the bottom of the box. "Maybe that would attract more attention."

"I know," agreed Lisa, rubbing her hands to keep them warm. "We've got to do something. I'm going to have to go in a few minutes, and we've only gotten one dollar."

"When are you relatives arriving?" Carole asked.

Maybe if they talked about something else for a while their collection problems wouldn't seem so bad.

"Late this afternoon." Lisa rolled her eyes and sighed.

"Did you and your mother get everything baked?" asked Stevie.

Lisa nodded. "I think we must have baked everything that's ever been invented to bake in Scotland. Plus, we've cleaned the house from top to bottom, until it shines. Our house could be a five-star hotel!"

Carole frowned. "Are your relatives real picky?"

"I don't think so. I haven't seen them in years, but they used to be just regular, normal people. I think my mother's just gone off the deep end, as usual." All the girls knew that Mrs. Atwood often worked overly hard at getting things as close to perfect as possible.

"Do they have any kids?" Stevie asked.

"They have two sons, Eliot and Douglas, who are about our age, and twin baby girls whom I've never met. Since I'm in charge of entertaining Eliot and Douglas, I thought I'd bring them over to Pine Hollow so you guys could meet them. They're really nice."

Stevie snickered. "Do they wear kilts and dance those jigs?"

"I don't think so." Lisa shook her head. "Mom is pretty sure they wear jeans."

"Good," said Carole. "Then we can take them riding."

Just then a car pulled up beside the curb. "Hi, girls!"

123

Mrs. Atwood called as she rolled down her window. "How's it going?"

"Fine, Mrs. Atwood," Carole and Stevie called together.

"Lisa, you need to come home now. The Rosses are on the way," Mrs. Atwood said.

Lisa got up from her chair. "Bye, guys. Sorry I have to leave. Good luck with the toy campaign. I'll see you in a couple of days."

"Bye, Lisa," Stevie said. "Thanks for all your help."

They sat there and watched as Mrs. Atwood drove away. "Gosh," Carole sighed. "It feels like it's getting colder."

"I know." Stevie rubbed her arms to keep warm. "Why don't I go get us some hot chocolate? My mom gave me some extra money in case we got cold."

"That would be great, Stevie." Carole smiled.

Stevie disappeared into TD's. A few more people passed by Carole and the big box. All were sorry the Marines' toys had been stolen, but everyone seemed to be in a hurry—rushing around to get their own Christmas errands accomplished. By the time Stevie returned with two cups of hot chocolate, Carole had collected only ten more dollars.

"I don't think we're going to have a hundred dollars by the end of the day," Carole announced sadly as Stevie handed her a cup. "I don't think we're even going to have twenty-five dollars."

"This is terrible," said Stevie. "I don't understand. Everybody's sorry the toys were stolen, but nobody wants to do anything about it."

"I think people are just too caught up in their own business." Carole blew on her hot chocolate. "I mean they're all buying presents or buying wrapping paper or going to the supermarket to get stuff for Christmas meals. It's like they want to help, but they just don't have the time."

Stevie took a sip of her hot chocolate. "Maybe this afternoon isn't such a great afternoon. I mean, maybe tomorrow afternoon will be better. And Saturday. Everybody's in a good mood on Saturdays."

The girls sat and drank their hot chocolate. Carole thought about how disappointed her father would be when she came home and told him that they'd collected only eleven dollars all day. She knew he would be very proud of them for trying, but she wanted to show him that The Saddle Club could make an important contribution. The sun was sinking low in the sky and a cold wind had started to blow from the west when Stevie tapped her on the shoulder.

"I don't know about you," Stevie began, "but I'm freezing." She peeked inside the box. "We've gotten eleven dollars so far. What do you say we call it quits for today and start again tomorrow afternoon? My mom should be here in a few minutes, anyway."

"Okay," Carole said resignedly. She looked at Stevie.

Her cheeks were bright pink. "Maybe everybody will be more in the Christmas spirit tomorrow."

They stood up and began folding their chairs. Suddenly they heard footsteps hurrying along the sidewalk behind them. "Why, what's this?" a voice asked. "Is somebody giving away kittens?"

They turned around. An elderly woman stood there, peering into the box. She was dressed in baggy, paint-spattered jeans and a rumpled, dirty-looking coat. Battered tennis shoes with unmatched laces were tied on her feet, and she wore a green stocking cap pulled down to her ears. She looked quizzically up at Carole and Stevie through thick glasses. "There aren't any kittens in here! Just money."

"Oh, no, ma'am," Carole explained quickly. "We're not giving away kittens. We're trying to collect money to replace the toys that were stolen from the Marines' toy drive warehouse."

"Stolen?" The woman blinked. Her eyes were pale blue. "When?"

"Two nights ago," said Stevie. "You may have seen my friend Carole here on television. She was in the paper, too."

"No, I don't have a television, and I haven't taken the paper in years." The woman chirped a little birdlike laugh. "There's too much bad news to read about these days, anyway. I've heard it can raise your blood pressure to dangerous levels!"

126

Stevie and Carole exchanged a quick glance. This was one of the strangest conversations they'd ever had.

"You say somebody stole all the Marines' toys?" she asked again. "What are the Marines doing with toys, anyway? They're grown men!"

"Yes, ma'am," Carole replied. "But every year the Marines collect toys for all the needy children in the area. This year somebody broke into their warehouse and stole all the toys. If we don't help, none of these children will have anything for Christmas."

"Oh, how terrible." The old woman's blue eyes softened with concern. For a moment she looked as if she might cry. "I can't think of anything worse than some little child not getting anything for Christmas." She wasn't carrying a purse, so she dug down into the pocket of her jeans. She pulled out a key, a wadded-up tissue, and two dollar bills.

"Here," she said, dropping one of the bills into Stevie and Carole's box. "Take this. It's not much, but it might help some." She gave an apologetic smile. "Everybody deserves something at Christmas."

"But—" Stevie began.

"Merry Christmas to you, girls," the old woman said, hurrying away. "I've got to hurry and catch my bus."

"Thank you!" Stevie and Carole called together. They watched as the woman hurried off, whistling and talking to herself. She walked to the bus stop, said something to the person in the Santa Claus suit ringing the bell, and

127

sat down on a bench. In a moment the bus pulled up. The doors opened and the woman climbed on. She waved to Stevie and Carole as the bus passed by and pulled into the late-afternoon traffic.

"Gosh," said Stevie, waving back. "I was going to give her dollar back to her. She's probably on some senior citizen gift list herself."

"I know," Carole agreed. "Do you think she's homeless? I can't imagine that anybody who had a real home would be out dressed like that."

Stevie shook her head. "I don't know. She sure doesn't look like she has a lot of money."

Carole swallowed hard. "I know. And she gave half of what little she had to buy toys for needy children. And that woman who was wearing a fancy fur coat didn't give us a dime."

"That's really something," said Stevie, shaking her head as the bus carrying the old woman pulled away into the cold afternoon.

14

"YEEEEOOOOOOWWWWWW!" THE SHRIEK rang through the Atwoods' house, all the way into the kitchen.

"Good grief!" cried Lisa, her eyes wide. "What was that?"

"One of the twins, I imagine." Mrs. Atwood shoved the brownish mound of haggis into the oven for its final baking. She turned to Lisa, her face flushed from the heat of the stove. "Why don't you go see what everybody's doing and then come back and help me get everything on the table?"

"Okay, Mom." Lisa hung up the dish towel she was carrying.

"And make sure everybody has everything they need, Lisa. The boys might want something to eat or drink. They've all had a terribly long flight."

"Okay, Mom," Lisa repeated. She walked out of the kitchen and turned down the hall, immediately bumping into Sarah Ross, her mother's cousin.

"Pardon me, dear," Sarah said with a warm smile. "I was just coming to see if I could help your mum in the kitchen."

"That's okay," Lisa said. "I was just coming to see if I could help whoever screamed."

Sarah laughed. "Oh, that was just Caitlin. Seems that Fiona was quite taken with Caitlin's new Big Bird toy and wanted it for herself. They had a bit of a row, but James is sorting them out." Sarah smiled. "Why don't you go have a chat with Eliot and Dougie, and I'll help your mum."

"Thanks," said Lisa. "I'm sure she'd love it."

She walked into the den. Eliot and Douglas sat with Lisa's dad on the sofa, watching a football game that blared from the television. James Ross sat on the floor in front of the crackling fire, holding little Fiona in his lap. Both of the twins were crying, their faces almost as red as their hair. They took one look at Lisa and cried even more loudly.

"Gosh," Lisa said. "I hope I'm not scaring them."

"Oh, you're not," James assured her. "They're just out of sorts from the flight, and everything is strange to them."

"Do you think they might like something to eat?" Lisa raised her voice so that James could hear her above the din. The twins continued to squawk, and Caitlin's face was so red she looked as if she might pop.

James smiled up at Lisa. "Well, a biscuit might be nice. It's been quite a while since they've eaten."

"I'm sorry, but I don't think my mom's baked any biscuits," Lisa apologized. Inwardly she groaned. Biscuits were the only thing she and her mother hadn't baked.

James laughed and shook his head. "I think I meant to say a saltine. A flat, crispy square of highly toasted bread. We call them biscuits in Scotland."

"Oh." Lisa frowned. "You mean a cracker?"

"I think so." James nodded.

"Just a minute, then." She hurried into the kitchen, put several crackers on a plate, and brought them back to the den. "Something like this?" she asked, holding the plate out to James.

"Exactly," James said delightedly. "Biscuits!"

He gave one cracker to each of the twins. Immediately they stopped crying and began to munch away. "Well." James smiled up at Lisa again. "Maybe all they were was hungry."

"I'm sure we'll eat in just a few minutes," Lisa assured him. "Mother's fixed a wonderful haggis."

Suddenly a roar went up from Eliot and Douglas on the sofa. Whatever team they were watching had just scored a touchdown.

"All right!" Eliot raised his arms triumphantly above his head.

"Smashing run!" Douglas cried.

"They've finally got a quarterback who can throw the ball," said Lisa's father with a grin. "The Redskins could go all the way to the Super Bowl this year."

"I'd love to see that," said Douglas.

"Me too," Eliot chimed in.

Lisa looked at the two boys sitting on the sofa. Douglas had red hair like the twins, while Eliot's hair was blond, like his mother's. Both had rosy cheeks and blue eyes that twinkled when they laughed, and they dressed just like American teenagers—in jeans, sneakers, and T-shirts. Lisa sat down on the arm of the sofa. Since she knew her mother expected her to entertain her cousins, she'd been looking at books on soccer and curling and rugby, sports that were popular in Scotland.

"How are the soccer teams doing in Scotland now?" she asked.

"The what?" Douglas gave her a blank look.

"The soccer teams," Lisa repeated. "You know, soccer?" She kicked at an imaginary ball with her right foot.

Eliot frowned and shook his head. "I'm sorry, Lisa. I'm not sure what you're talking about."

"Soccer," Lisa said more loudly. "You try to make goals with a round ball. You can kick it or bounce it off your head, but you can't touch it with your hands."

"Oh!" Douglas cried. "Football!"

"No." Lisa shook her head and pointed at the TV set.

"Football is what you're watching on television. Soccer is what you guys are supposed to play in Scotland!"

Suddenly everyone in the room began to laugh. Lisa sat there blinking. Had they all gone crazy? Didn't anyone in Scotland speak English?

"Oh, Lisa," James laughed. "Please don't look so confused! It's just that in most of the world soccer is known as football. Only you Yanks call it soccer!"

Lisa blinked. "Then what do you call the sport with the oblong ball that those two teams are now playing on the screen?"

"It's football, too," James explained. "But it's called American football. It's become quite popular in the United Kingdom."

"It has," said Douglas. "Everyone's quite keen on it at home. We went to an exhibition match in Glasgow. The Atlanta Falcons played the . . ."

"New York Mets," Eliot finished.

"The New York Jets," Lisa's father corrected. "The Mets are one of New York's baseball teams."

"Sorry," said Eliot, his cheeks growing even pinker. "Anyway, it was a lark."

Suddenly the crowd on television roared. Everyone on the sofa turned their attention back to the game. A player had caught the ball with one hand and was running down the field, shaking off tacklers as he went.

"Go!" shrieked Douglas.

"Play up!" yelled Eliot just as loudly. "Stout lad!"

Lisa got up from the sofa and went back to the kitchen. She shook her head. As much as she liked Eliot and Douglas and wanted to get to know them better, it seemed as if they were speaking a different language. She sighed. Maybe she'd have better luck in the kitchen. Sarah Ross might actually call a pot a pot, and a pan might still be known as a pan.

"Oh, Lisa, I'm glad you're back." Mrs. Atwood turned away from the stove and gave Lisa a hurried smile. "If you'll carry this bowl of turnips to the table and light the candles, then we'll be ready to eat."

"These 'nips here?" Sarah Ross asked, holding up a china bowl.

Mrs. Atwood nodded. "I used Grandmother Ross's recipe."

"I'll take them in," said Sarah. "They smell delicious. I've haven't had 'nips in ages!"

Lisa looked at her mother curiously as Sarah carried the dish into the dining room. "Didn't you say they ate turnips all the time?" she asked in whisper.

Mrs. Atwood shrugged. "I thought they did." She took off her apron. "Well, let's go eat. I know everyone must be starved!"

They ate in the Atwoods' dining room, and for a little while everything was calm. The television set was turned off, the twins weren't crying, and everyone sat around the candlelit table chatting about the Rosses' plans for their visit in America.

"This is extraordinary haggis, Eleanor." James Ross cleared his throat as he complimented Mrs. Atwood. "I don't believe I've eaten like this in years."

Mrs. Atwood gave an uneasy smile. "Really? I thought Scots ate haggis a lot."

"Oh, no," said Sarah Ross. "I don't think any of us have had haggis since Hogmanay 1984."

"Hogmanay?" Lisa asked as she pretended to swallow a bite of the haggis. She was almost afraid to ask what Hogmanay was. If soccer was football and crackers were biscuits, then Hogmanay must be some sort of ritual that had something to do with pigs!

"Yes. Hogmanay." Sarah looked at Lisa, then laughed. "New Year's Eve."

"Oh, I see," said Lisa, becoming more confused than ever. Her mother shouldn't have given her books about Scottish sports to read. She should have given her a Scottish dictionary just so she could figure out what the Rosses were talking about!

Just then Caitlin gave a yelp. Everyone turned to the twins. Fiona had taken a fistful of haggis and had smeared it all over Caitlin's forehead! Fiona was shrieking with glee, while Caitlin was just plain shrieking.

"Oh, Fiona!" Sarah swooped toward Caitlin. "Naughty girl!" Just as she was reaching over to wipe Caitlin's face

135

with her napkin, she accidentally bumped a full glass of water with her elbow. The glass teetered for an instant, then spilled all over Mrs. Atwood's good linen tablecloth.

"Oh, no!" James cried. He leaped up from his chair and began to blot the water with his napkin. "Boys," he said to Douglas and Eliot. "Help, here!"

The boys jumped up to help their father. The Atwoods jumped up to remove the haggis platter. Lisa jumped up to help whoever needed help. In an instant their nice quiet dinner had turned into bedlam, with everybody standing up blotting water or removing dishes or trying to wipe Caitlin's face.

"I'm so sorry, Eleanor," Sarah said, handing Caitlin to James and helping Mrs. Atwood dry off the table. "I'm a clumsy lummox!"

"Oh, don't apologize," said Mrs. Atwood. "Accidents happen." She gave one quick, mournful glance at her once beautiful table, then smiled. "Why don't we eat dessert in the den? I'll serve the plates in the kitchen and we can eat in front of the fire."

"Jolly good plan," said James, still wiping bits of haggis from Caitlin's face.

Everyone relocated to the den. Mr. Atwood turned the television set back on, and soon Eliot and Douglas and James were clustered in front of another football game. Mrs. Atwood and Sarah sat in front of the fire planning a trip to the National Gallery in Washington, while Caitlin and Fiona took turns bonking each other on the head

136

with a red plastic hammer. Lisa sat on the sofa and watched everything. The party seemed to be swirling around her. Finally she stood up.

"Mom, if it's okay with you, I think I'll go to bed," she said, barely hiding a yawn. It had been a long day for her. She'd gone to school, then had helped Carole and Stevie at the toy collection booth. After that she had mostly tried to figure out what her Scottish cousins were trying to say. Suddenly all she longed for was a little peace and quiet.

"Have you shown Douglas and Eliot where everything is?" Mrs. Atwood asked.

"Yes," Lisa replied. "They know where to find anything they need."

"Good. Then sleep well, dear." Mrs. Atwood gave her a warm smile.

"Thanks for all your help, Lisa," Sarah Ross added. "You've been a wonderful host."

"Thanks," Lisa said, this time with a yawn. "I'll see you guys tomorrow."

She walked upstairs, longing for the quiet of her own room. *This must be how Max feels at the stable*, she thought as she opened her bedroom door. *There's Deborah and Maxi and Mrs. Reg and Red O'Malley and all the horses and all the riders.* Lisa gave another big yawn as she collapsed onto her bed. *No wonder he looks so tired all the time!*

"Brrreeeeeeaaaaackkkkkkk." Lisa's eyelids flew open. For an instant she didn't know where she was. All she knew was that something, somewhere, was being horribly murdered!

"*Brrreeeeeeaaaaackkkkkkkk!*" The noise rang out again. She blinked. Suddenly the room came into focus and she realized that she was in her bedroom, in her own bed. But what was that awful noise?

"*Wwwrrraaaaannggghhh!*" Now the noise was different, worse somehow. She got up and threw on her robe. She couldn't imagine how, but somebody was downstairs in her house killing some helpless animal.

"Stop!" she yelled as she raced down the stairs. "Whatever you're doing, stop!"

She hurried into the living room, but no one was

there. She ran down the hall, but it, too, was empty. *"Wwwrrraaaaaannggghhh!"* The noise rang out again, this time from the den. Whatever slaughter was taking place was happening in there! She ran as fast as she could and flung open the door. There, standing with one foot resting on the raised hearth, was Eliot. Cradled in his arms was not some helpless animal, but a set of plaid bagpipes!

"Morning, Lisa!" he said cheerily.

Lisa blinked. "Are you the one making that awful noise?"

Eliot frowned. "What awful noise?"

"That loud agonized wailing that sounds like a goose is being strangled," Lisa replied.

Eliot's cheeks grew red. "Well, uh, yes, I guess I am." He lowered the pipes and shrugged. "I'm a piper in the Clan Ross Pipe Band at home, and it's important that we stay in practice. I'm sorry. I thought my mum told you I would need to practice."

"No." Lisa gave a relieved sigh. "I guess that was one little detail she must have forgotten to mention." For a long moment, Eliot and Lisa just looked at each other. Then they both began to laugh.

"I'm sorry," Lisa giggled. "But you looked so surprised when I came in here and found you with that thing."

"I'm sorry, too," laughed Eliot. "I didn't expect you'd come bursting in here in your nightgown trying to save a goose from certain death!"

They laughed until Mrs. Atwood and Sarah Ross came into the den.

"What's so funny?" asked Lisa's mom. "We heard you laughing all the way in the kitchen."

"Oh, Mom, don't ask," said Lisa, wiping the tears from her eyes. "Let's just say that my appreciation of Scottish music has grown overnight."

"Well, why don't you both come and get some break-fast and we can talk about what we're going to do today."

Eliot and Lisa walked into the kitchen, where everyone else was sitting around the table eating breakfast. Mrs. Atwood had fixed oatcakes and kippers, little smoked fish that everyone ate in Scotland. Skipping the dark-colored kippers, Lisa grabbed an oatcake and sat down between Douglas and James.

"Okay, Lisa, here's the plan for today." Mrs. Atwood looked at Lisa and smiled. "Your father got four tickets for the football game this afternoon, but it doesn't start until three. Sarah and I want to take the twins shopping while your father and James look at some new computer equip-ment. That leaves Douglas and Eliot with nothing to do until the game. Can you think of some activity you three might enjoy together?"

"I could take them to Pine Hollow," Lisa suggested. She looked at Eliot. "That is, if Eliot can tear himself away from his bagpipes."

"What's Pine Hollow?" Eliot asked with a laugh. "I don't want to jump into anything rash."

"Pine Hollow's a stable. I ride there at least three times a week," explained Lisa. "They've got lots of horses and beautiful trails."

"Sure," said Eliot. "I could put my pipes down for that."

"Okay, then." Mrs. Atwood smiled. "Lisa, why don't you three walk over to Pine Hollow, and then you can take the boys over to TD's for a treat. We'll pick you up there just in time for the game."

"Great," said Lisa. "That's the best idea I've heard all morning."

Later, after their parents had gone off on their own adventures, Lisa and Douglas and Eliot walked up the curving road to Pine Hollow. The air was cold, and their footsteps echoed on the pavement.

"Do you guys ride horses in Scotland?" Lisa asked as they neared the stable.

Eliot shook his head. "Mum used to a little, but there's only one old horse in our entire town, and he only gives rides to little children in the summertime."

"Looks like there's more little children in that one riding ring than in our entire town." Douglas pointed to the front paddock, where Max was conducting a class of about twenty very beginning riders.

"Actually, that's a bigger than normal class," Lisa said. "Max has been awfully busy lately." She walked faster. "Come on. I want to introduce you to everybody."

They entered the warm dimness of the stable. Lisa felt

good to be at Pine Hollow again. She loved the sweet smells of saddle soap and hay and the soft sound of horses eating. She'd been so busy helping her mother at home and Stevie and Lisa with the toy drive that it seemed as if she hadn't seen Prancer in months, although it had really been only a couple of days. She introduced her cousins to Mrs. Reg and Red O'Malley, then pulled them down one aisle. "Come this way and I'll introduce you to the horses."

"This is my friend Stevie Lake's horse, Belle," she said, stopping in front of Belle's stall. Belle was eating, but she poked her head over the stall door and gave Lisa a friendly nicker through a mouthful of hay.

"She's pretty," Eliot said. "Does she always talk with her mouth full?"

"Actually, she does," Lisa said with a chuckle. "It's a habit she gets from her owner."

Just then Starlight stuck his head over his stall door and gave a loud whinny. "This is Starlight," Lisa said, moving on to the next stall. "He belongs to my friend Carole Hanson, who knows more about horses than anybody. All three of us have a club together, called The Saddle Club."

"How does one join?" asked Douglas.

"Well, it's pretty easy. All you have to be is willing to help the other club members out at all times and be crazy about horses."

"How about just plain daft?" asked Eliot with a grin.

"Huh?" Lisa frowned.

"He means crazy," Douglas translated for his brother.

"Well, that, too, I suppose." Lisa laughed. "Come on down this way. I want to show you the horse I ride all the time."

They walked past several stalls until they reached Prancer. The big bay mare was slurping water when they stuck their heads over her door.

"Hi, Prancer," Lisa called softly. "Hi, girl!"

Prancer looked up with a dripping chin and nuzzled Lisa's head. Lisa patted her neck, which felt surprisingly warm. "Gosh, Prancer, you feel like you've just been ridden!" she said.

"Is no one else supposed to ride her?" Eliot rubbed Prancer on her nose.

"Well, no," Lisa replied. "She's a schooling horse, so anybody who takes a lesson here can ride her, but Max doesn't usually use her on Saturday morning."

"She's quite lovely," said Douglas. He scratched Prancer behind her ears. "Maybe someone came along and saw her and just had to ride her."

"I suppose." Lisa sighed. Most of the time she considered Prancer her horse. Times like this reminded her that Prancer belonged to the stable, not to her, and that always made her a little sad. "Anyway," she said, giving Prancer a final pat, "I ride her most of the time, and I'm sure she likes me riding her the best!"

"Absolutely," agreed Eliot.

Lisa showed Douglas and Eliot the rest of the stable. They touched the lucky horseshoe and walked up the hill to where all the trails began. Then Lisa realized that it was time to take them to TD's.

"I guess you'll have to meet Max some other time," she said as they hurried back through the stable and out to the road beyond. "Maybe we can come back in a day or two and take a trail ride."

"That would be super!" Douglas said. "Almost as much fun as football!"

They walked through the cold bright air to the shopping center. The parking lot was crowded with cars, and Lisa could see Stevie and Carole tending their toy drive box in front of TD's.

"Oh, good," she said as she and Eliot and Douglas crossed the street. "You can meet my friends Stevie and Carole. They're the ones sitting behind that big cardboard box."

"Is this some sort of new American craze?" teased Eliot. "Box-sitting?"

"No," giggled Lisa. "We're helping collect toys for needy kids at Christmas. Someone stole all the toys the Marines had already collected."

Douglas frowned. "That's a pretty shoddy thing to do."

"I know," Lisa agreed. "And Carole's father was in charge of the whole thing."

Just then Stevie stood up and waved. "Hi, Lisa! Come on over!"

144

Lisa waved as she and her cousins hurried across the parking lot. "Hi, Stevie. Hi, Carole," she said as they stepped onto the sidewalk. "I'd like to introduce my cousins. Stevie and Carole, this is Eliot and Douglas Ross, from Glenochy, Scotland."

"Hi." Stevie grinned. "Welcome to the States."

"Hi," Carole said, smiling warmly at the guys.

"Hi, girls," Eliot and Douglas said together. "Lisa's told us a lot about you," added Eliot with a grin.

"Oh?" said Stevie. "Like what?"

"Let's see." Eliot squinted with one eye. "That Carole's the horse expert and you talk a lot, or is it that Carole talks a lot and you're the horse expert, or is it that you're horse daft, and she's all daft or maybe all of you are all daft?"

"Huh?" said Carole and Stevie together.

"Daft means crazy," explained Lisa with a laugh. "Eliot and Douglas speak something that sounds like English, but it isn't really. It's some kind of weird language where all the words mean something else."

Stevie grinned at the two boys and spoke slowly. "Do you know what the word *ice cream* means?"

Douglas winked. "Does it mean a frozen dairy product that's served in a dish or a cone with all sorts of delicious stuff on top?"

"Yes!" Stevie cried. "You've got it! We're communicating!"

"Then I vote that we take a break from the toy campaign and go inside TD's and get some ice cream," said Carole with a shiver. "I'm so cold right now that ice cream might even warm me up!"

They pulled their box and sign inside TD's and sat down at their favorite booth. Their usual waitress soon made her way to the table with her order pad.

"What'll it be today, folks?" she said, her pencil poised.

"Uh, I'll have hot chocolate with extra marshmallows," said Carole.

"Me too," said Lisa.

"Me three," said Douglas, blowing on his cold fingers.

The waitress scribbled on her pad, then turned to Stevie. "Your Christmas special?" she asked.

Stevie frowned for a moment. "No, today I think I'll have chocolate ice cream with pineapple sauce and red cherries on top, with just a little dab of marshmallow on the side."

"Gosh," Eliot said. "That sounds delicious." He looked up at the waitress. "Could you make that two?"

The waitress looked at him as if he were as crazy as Stevie, but turned back to the counter to fill their orders.

"Do you like weird ice cream, too?" Stevie asked Eliot, her eyes bright.

He nodded. "The weirder the better."

"Oh, brother," said Lisa. "This could turn out to be a dangerous combination!"

"Anything that has to do with Eliot and ice cream can be dangerous," said Douglas with a grin.

In a moment the waitress brought their orders. She placed three cups of hot cocoa on the table, then two dishes of a dark brown and yellow creation.

"Mmmmm," said Stevie after she'd taken her first bite.

"Jolly good," agreed Eliot, smiling. "Your instincts were perfect!"

"Yucchhh!" said Lisa and Carole and Douglas together as they sipped their hot chocolate.

"So what have you guys got planned for your trip to the States?" Carole asked as Eliot dug into his ice cream.

"Well, this afternoon we're going to an American football game," he answered eagerly. "Then Mom wants us to go to the National Gallery, then Dad wants us to see the Smithsonian . . ."

"Then Lisa wants to take us horseback riding," added Douglas.

"Wow," said Stevie. "Sounds like you're going to have a busy trip."

"I know." Eliot scraped up some pineapple sauce. "Somewhere in there we'll have to fit Christmas in, too, I expect."

"Oh, look," said Lisa, peering out the window. "There's my dad and James. I think it's time for you guys to go to the game."

"Good timing." Eliot wiped his mouth with a paper napkin. "I'd just finished." He pulled out some British money from his pocket. "Will five pounds do?"

Lisa shook her head. "I don't think TD's takes British money. You guys get going. My mom gave me some money to pay."

"Thanks," said Douglas, finishing his cocoa in one gulp. He and his brother slid out of the booth. "Well, ladies, it's been a pleasure. Hope to see you daft girls again soon."

"Daft is as daft does," replied Stevie with a grin.

"Cheers!" said Eliot as he and Douglas hurried out the door and into the car. "Catch you later!"

The girls watched as the car pulled away from the curb. "They're nice," said Stevie. "I like them. Eliot has great taste in ice cream."

"They're both cute, too," added Carole. "I love their accents."

"They are nice guys," said Lisa. "You should hear Eliot play the bagpipes."

"What does he sound like?" asked Carole.

Lisa shuddered. "It's an experience you won't soon forget." She took a sip of cocoa. "Hey, how's the toy collecting? Have you guys gotten a lot of money today?"

Stevie looked at Carole and gave a disappointed sigh. "No," she replied. "It's not going well at all. We've been out here all day and we've only collected nineteen dollars."

"Gosh," said Lisa. "Is that all?"

Carole nodded. "People come by and say they're sorry the toys were stolen, but it seems like nobody has any

148

money to spare. Either that or they're too busy with their own errands to get involved." She stared at the table. "My dad's going to be so disappointed!"

"Maybe we should rethink this," Stevie suggested. "Maybe it's time to try something else."

"But, Stevie, it's so close to Christmas," Carole cried. "What could we possibly come up with now?"

"I don't know," said Stevie. "But let's each concentrate on it for a whole minute, starting right now!" Stevie stared into her empty ice cream dish. Carole and Lisa stared into their cups. For a moment no one spoke. Then Stevie snapped her fingers.

"I've got it!" she cried. "It's absolutely fail-proof!"

"What?" Lisa and Carole asked together.

"Let's all go Christmas caroling door to door and ask people for donations along the way! We can get a bunch of kids from Pine Hollow to join us. We'll practice the carols, then canvass the neighborhood and ask for money for toys for needy children after we sing. People can't turn us down if we're standing there caroling at their front door!"

"I don't know, Stevie," Lisa said. "People might hear us singing and not even open the front door."

"No, they won't," Stevie insisted. "We'll be great. I've taken so many singing lessons from Ms. Bennefield that I sing like a bird. People will just have to give us lots of money!"

"I'm not so sure about that, Stevie," said Carole. "But I

have to admit it's the only other plan we've been able to come up with, and we're running out of time."

"Okay," said Stevie. "When we get home we'll divide up the list of Pine Hollow riders. We'll tell everybody what's going on, and we'll have just enough time to practice our carols the day after tomorrow."

"Well." Carole shrugged. "I guess we've got nothing to lose." She looked at Stevie and smiled. "Do you want to call Veronica or shall I?"

"Oh, I'll call her," replied Stevie sweetly. "I just haven't decided exactly what to call her yet!"

16

"OKAY, PRANCER, REMEMBER how much fun this was yesterday?" Carole looked over her shoulder at the big bay mare as she splashed in the creek. Prancer watched from the bank, her eyes and ears alert. "In just a few minutes, we're going to do this together." Carole did a little tap dance in the creek, kicking water up to the top of her boots. Prancer lowered her head and sniffed the water curiously. "See?" Carole said. "It's just water. Nothing to be afraid of!"

Prancer's nose quivered. Slowly she put her right front foot in the water. "Good girl!" said Carole. "Now put your other foot in, and we can have some fun."

The big horse looked at Carole once more, then put her other front foot in the water. Carole backed up a step, and Prancer followed. Soon they were both standing in the middle of the creek.

"Good girl!" Carole praised Prancer and patted her neck. "Let's just play around out here a minute so you can be sure there's nothing to be afraid of."

Carole splashed gently in the creek, making sure not to kick the water anywhere near Prancer's face. Prancer eyed the water suspiciously for a moment. Then, as the little drops of water fell harmlessly on her legs, she began to relax.

"Wonderful, Prancer!" Carole cried. "Now follow me." Carole backed all the way across the creek, keeping her eyes on Prancer. The horse hesitated for a moment, then followed Carole willingly, climbing out of the creek on the other side.

"Good job, girl!" Carole rubbed Prancer's nose. This new training method she'd read about was really working. Just a few more sessions like this and Prancer could be leaping through the water like a trout.

"Okay, let's cross once more and we'll be done for the day." Carole slowly waded back into the creek. This time she didn't look at Prancer but just walked across the creek as if she expected Prancer to follow. Sure enough, midway across the creek she heard the deep splash of a horse hoof being plunked down in the water. It was working! Prancer was almost cured!

Carole climbed out of the water. Prancer followed, looking at her expectantly, as if to ask, "What next?"

"Lesson's over for today, Prancer," Carole said, laughing as she climbed back up in the saddle. "Now I've got to sneak you back inside the stable before Lisa finds out we're gone." She tightened her legs around Prancer. "Let's go! And trot as quietly as you can!"

In just a few minutes they crested the hill above Pine Hollow. Carole could see the riders hurrying inside for their lesson. That meant Lisa was probably already there. Quickly she dismounted and led Prancer through the back entrance to the stable. If everything was going as they'd planned, Stevie would have Lisa occupied in the tack room. Quietly Carole led Prancer past the door and took a quick glance inside. Just as she had thought, Stevie and Lisa were inside polishing tack, their heads bent over their work.

"How come you're polishing Veronica's saddle, Stevie?" Lisa asked, looking up from the bridle she was cleaning.

"Well, she dumped it right here, and it seemed a shame to leave it all dirty." Stevie fingered the stitching on the expensive saddle. "It's terrible not to take care of your equipment better than this."

"But I thought you were plotting a big revenge on Veronica," said Lisa.

"Well, I was. But I got so involved in the toy drive that I sort of forgot about it." Stevie rubbed harder on the saddle. "It's odd, but it feels kind of good to do something nice for her."

Suddenly a shadow fell between them. "What are you doing to that saddle?" a hard, angry voice called out.

Stevie looked up. Veronica stood there, her green eyes flashing.

"I was just giving it a good cleaning," explained Stevie. "I know you've been busy lately with play practice, and you haven't had a lot of time to take care of your tack." Stevie smiled. "I cleaned your bridle, too."

"My what?" Veronica snatched the bridle from the bench where Stevie had placed it. She began to check all the straps and buckles to make sure they were still tight. When she found that the bridle was just as she had left it, only cleaner, she looked at Stevie.

"Hmpf!" she snorted, giving Stevie a suspicious look. "You haven't been tampering with any more of my equipment, have you?"

"Well, I did wipe some mud off your boots," Stevie said sweetly.

Veronica stomped across the room and grabbed her boots from her locker. Though they gleamed spotlessly in the bright light, she turned each one upside down and shook it, as if expecting something awful to fall out. When nothing did, she put the boots back.

"I don't know what you're up to, Stevie Lake, but if you damage my property in any way my father will sue you!"

Stevie held out her hands. "Hey, I'm just trying to be helpful. After all, it's Christmas!"

"Yeah, right," Veronica snarled. She turned on her heel

and stormed out the door. Stevie and Lisa listened as her angry footsteps echoed down the stable aisle. Lisa turned to Stevie and frowned.

"Are you sure this isn't a part of some revenge you've dreamed up?" she asked. "Veronica seems to get more upset the nicer you are to her."

"I know." Stevie looked at Lisa innocently, then smiled slyly. "It almost works better, doesn't it? My being nice seems to get under her skin a lot more than any of my usual tricks. She looks like she's about to have some kind of nervous conniption!"

Just then Carole burst into the room. "Hi, guys!" she called breathlessly.

"Carole!" Lisa said. "Where have you been? Stevie and I have been cleaning tack for hours."

"I had to catch up on some Christmas errands," Carole explained. "It was the only chance I had to get them done. We'd better hurry and tack up. Class is about to begin."

"There's no need for me to hurry," said Lisa. "Every time I've ridden Prancer lately, she's already warm. Max must be giving somebody a lot of extra lessons on her. All I'll need to do is saddle her up and we'll be ready to go."

Stevie stood up. "Well, let's hurry anyway. I need to ask Max if I can remind the class about the Christmas carol practice tomorrow afternoon."

They hurried on out to their horses, tacking them up quickly. Just as Lisa had expected, Prancer was warm, and looked almost surprised to find that she was going to be tacked up again so soon.

"See what I mean?" Lisa said to Carole as they led their horses toward the indoor riding ring. She gave Prancer's warm shoulder a pat. "Prancer's already been ridden today. When I went to her stall she looked like she might even be ready for a nap!"

"Max must have another dedicated student, then," Carole replied, trying hard to hide her smile.

When they reached the ring Stevie was already there, talking to Max. Max again carried baby Maxi on his shoulders and a cell phone in his left hand.

"Poor Max," said Carole as they took their places. "I've never seen him this busy. He's got to take care of Maxi, take calls for the stable, and teach a class at the same time."

"He must feel like I do at home," said Lisa. "That's when I have to help my mom, entertain Douglas and Eliot, and translate Scottish into English all at once!"

Just then Stevie quit talking to Max and led Belle over between Prancer and Starlight.

"Did Max say you could make your announcement?" asked Carole.

Stevie nodded. "He said I'd have to make it quick, because he's got another class coming in right after ours."

"Hey, would it be okay if I brought Eliot and Douglas to practice tomorrow?" Lisa asked. "I'm supposed to entertain them while they're here, and they might enjoy

156

coming. I'm sure they must sing Christmas carols in Scotland, although I can't imagine what they call them."

"Sure." Stevie grinned. "The more the merrier. I'm going to invite Phil. Maybe he can teach us some Hanukkah songs."

"I can teach everybody the Kwanzaa song my mom taught me," Carole volunteered.

"Great," said Stevie as the three girls gathered their reins and mounted up. "This will be the most multicultural group of carolers Willow Creek has ever had!"

THE NEXT AFTERNOON everyone met in front of Pine Hollow at four. The weather was cloudy and cold, and most of the riders from Horse Wise were bundled up in warm parkas. A familiar station wagon pulled up, and Stevie's boy-friend, Phil Marsten, and his best friend, A.J., climbed out.

"Hi, Stevie," Phil called. He grinned and gave her a big hug. "Are we supposed to practice our singing out here in the cold?"

"Hi, Phil." Stevie smiled. "Actually, I'm not sure where we're going to practice. We need to ask Max about it."

Just then Max and Maxi hurried past the entrance of the stable. "Are these the Pine Hollow carolers?" Max paused a moment as Maxi grinned delightedly at all the people from the front pack he used to carry her.

158

"Yes," said Carole. "And we need a place to practice. Preferably a warm place. It's kind of hard learning new songs in below-zero weather. Could we use the indoor ring?"

Max gave a sideways glance at Stevie. "How about the back tack room? The sound really carries from the indoor ring. I've heard how some of you sing before, and I don't want to put the horses off their feed."

"Oh, don't worry about me, Max," Stevie said with a grin. "I've taken voice lessons. I sing like an angel now."

"Well, practice in the back tack room anyway," said Max. "If you now sing like an angel, I don't want the horses to think they've all died and gone to heaven."

"Okay," said Stevie. "But I'm sure once you hear me you'll be amazed."

She and Carole led the crowd of carolers to the back tack room. They took off their hats and coats while Carole passed around sheets of paper with the words of seven Christmas carols.

"Where did you get those, Carole?" Stevie asked, looking at the neatly printed sheets.

"My dad took me down to his office last night and let me print them out on his computer. He said it was the least he could do, since we were doing this for the toy campaign."

"Hi, guys," a familiar voice said behind them. "Sorry we're late."

Stevie and Carole turned around. Lisa stood there, with Eliot and Douglas smiling behind her.

"Hi, Lisa," Carole said. "Hi, Eliot. Hi, Douglas. Glad you could make it. Lisa says you're going to teach us a Scottish Christmas carol."

"Oh, really?" Eliot looked surprised. "Funny, she didn't mention that to us."

"I guess I forgot," Lisa said sheepishly. "I was so busy helping Mom with the cock-a-leekie soup last night, and then we played darts until it was time to go to bed."

"Don't worry about it." Douglas laughed and nudged his brother. "I'm sure Mr. McBagpipes here can come up with something."

"Let's practice our old standbys first, and then we can learn some new ones," suggested Stevie.

"That sounds like a good idea," Carole agreed.

Lisa and her cousins joined everyone else in a big circle on the floor while Stevie stood up in front of the group. "Okay, guys," she began. "Does everyone here know the words to 'Jingle Bells'?"

Everyone nodded.

"Then let's start off with that one." Stevie stood up straight, took a deep breath, and launched into "Jingle Bells." Her voice rang out clear and on key. Stevie really had learned to sing! Everyone listened in astonishment for a moment, after which they joined in.

"Okay," said Stevie when they had finished. "That sounded pretty good."

"You sounded pretty good, too, Stevie," Phil called.

"Thanks." Stevie smiled at Phil's compliment. "What shall we sing next?"

"How about 'O Come, All Ye Faithful'?" said Jessica Adler.

"And then 'Joy to the World'," called May Grover. "That's my favorite."

"Okay," said Stevie. She led everyone through the carols Jessica and May had asked for. Then, just as the group started in on "Silent Night," there was a loud knock on the tack room door.

"What's going on in here?" Veronica appeared at the door, her normally pale skin flushed bright red. Everyone stopped singing and looked at her. She stared straight at Stevie. "Is this something you've plotted behind my back?"

Stevie blinked with surprise. "No, Veronica," she explained calmly. "We're practicing our carol singing for tomorrow night. I called you about it a couple of days ago, and I announced this practice at the end of riding class yesterday."

"She did, Veronica." Betsy Cavanaugh agreed with Stevie. "Why don't you come and sing with us? It's lots of fun."

"I'm sure it is." Veronica tossed her head. "But some of us don't have time to waste singing Christmas carols. Some of us wouldn't want to take the chance of running around the neighborhood and exposing our throats to the cold night air, particularly when some of us are starring in our school's Christmas play!"

"But . . . ," Stevie began.

Veronica turned and stormed off through the stable before anyone could say another word. Stevie watched her go, then shrugged and returned her attention to the carolers.

"Okay, what shall we sing next?" she asked.

"Let Eliot and Douglas teach us a traditional British carol now," called Lisa.

"Okay. Eliot and Douglas, now it's your turn." Stevie grinned as the two guys stood up. "Everybody, this is Eliot and Douglas Ross, Lisa's cousins from Scotland," she said as they came and stood beside her. "They say they sing Christmas carols in Scotland, but I've never heard any."

"Have you ever heard 'Child in a Manger'?" asked Eliot with a grin. "It's a favorite back home."

Stevie shook her head. "We'd all like to learn it, though."

"Okay. It goes like this." Eliot and Douglas both squared their shoulders as Stevie had and began to sing a lovely carol about a baby sleeping on Christmas morning. Everyone listened as the boys sang the first verse. The group joined in on the chorus. A few minutes later they sang the song all the way through, and by the time they had finished, everyone had learned a new carol.

"All right," said Stevie, clapping as the guys sat down.

"Thanks, Eliot and Douglas. That sounded great. Does anyone else have a carol they'd like to teach us?"

"I've got a Hanukkah song we could sing," said Phil, rising to his feet.

"Super," said Stevie. "Come on up here and teach us."

Phil stood up and sang a bouncy little song about candles shining in menorahs. All the carolers loved it, and in a few minutes they'd learned that one as well.

"Anybody else?" Stevie asked as Phil sat down.

"How about my Kwanzaa song?" said Carole.

"Sure," Stevie said.

Carole got up and stood beside Stevie. Everyone looked up at her, waiting for her to begin. She smiled. Suddenly she realized how wonderful it was that all these people were willing to help her raise money for her father's special project. They were all busy and didn't have to do it, but they were doing it to help her and people less fortunate. It would be her small gift to them in return to share the special song her mother had loved so.

"This is a song my mother taught me before she died," Carole said softly. "It's my favorite song, because it reminds me so much of her. It's about love and working hard together and being grateful for what the earth gives us."

Carole took a deep breath. She knew she hadn't had lessons as Stevie had, but she hoped she could sing the song well.

" 'We bring to this feast of Karamu, our colors of Kwanzaa love,' " she began. The words brought back wonderful memories of her mother, and it seemed to Carole that somehow her mother was right there with her. Everyone in the tack room was silent as Carole's song floated through the air. Stevie and Lisa looked at each other and smiled.

Suddenly Stevie caught sight of Deborah standing and listening at the tack room door. Deborah waited until Carole had finished her song, then motioned for Stevie to come to the door.

"What are you guys doing?" she whispered as Carole began to teach her song to the group. "You actually sound pretty good."

"We've been practicing Christmas carols, and now we're learning a Kwanzaa song." Stevie counted on her fingers. "So far we've learned a Hanukkah song and a Kwanzaa song and a bunch of traditional Christmas carols."

"That's wonderful." Deborah gave her a quizzical smile. "But are you doing this just for fun?"

"Oh, no. We're going Christmas caroling tomorrow night to raise money for the toy drive," Stevie explained. "We only collected nineteen dollars with our stand at TD's. We thought this would work out better. People can't turn us down if we're singing at their front door." Stevie grinned. "Plus, now we're an international, multicultural choral group!"

164

Deborah frowned. "What do you mean?"

"Lisa's cousins Eliot and Douglas are helping, too. They celebrate Christmas, but they're from Scotland. Phil's from here but he celebrates Hanukkah, and Carole celebrates Kwanzaa."

Deborah dug her reporter's notebook out of her purse and began to make notes. "Does Tress Montgomery know about this?"

"I don't think so. Carole's really crazy about getting a lot of money for the Marines, but I don't think she'd have the nerve to call Tress Montgomery."

Deborah opened her mouth to say something, but her cell phone rang. She answered it quickly, then tucked it back inside her purse. "Gotta go," she said to Stevie. "I've got to run down to the paper and then pick Max up here in an hour. Good luck with your caroling. I'll see you later!"

"Thanks," called Stevie as Deborah hurried off down the hall. She went back inside the tack room. Everyone had just finished singing Carole's song for the third time.

"That's a beautiful song, Carole," Meg Durham said. "Thanks for teaching it to us."

Stevie stood in front of the group again. "Okay, if everyone feels like they know the words to the carols, we'll meet here tomorrow evening at five, three hours before the Christmas party. That should give us lots of time to carol and make tons of money for the toy drive."

165

"Should we bring our words with us?" Someone waved the sheet Carole had passed out.

"Sure," said Stevie. "Don't forget to bring flashlights, too."

"Will we find out who our Secret Santas are at the party tomorrow night?" someone else asked as they all put on their coats.

"According to Max, we will," said Stevie.

"Good," said Jasmine James. "I can hardly wait."

"Okay, then," Stevie announced. "We'll see all you guys here tomorrow at five. Thanks for coming!"

Everyone crowded out the door. Phil and A.J. said they would see everyone tomorrow. Lisa and her cousins began to walk toward home.

"Do you really think we'll raise a lot of money, Stevie?" Carole asked as she zipped her parka up against the cold air.

"I know we will," Stevie said. "Don't you?"

"I hope so," said Carole, looking up into the dark sky and again sensing that somehow her mother was very close by. "I really hope so."

LISA WALKED TOWARD home between Eliot and Douglas. All the houses in her neighborhood had turned their Christmas lights on, and the whole street twinkled with a thousand different colors.

"I really enjoyed the carol practice, but who was that girl who stuck her head in the door and started blithering about being the star of some play?" Douglas asked as they hurried through the chilly darkness.

"That was Veronica diAngelo," Lisa said with exasperation. "She's the richest and snobbiest girl at Pine Hollow. And the hardest person to get along with, too. She's convinced Stevie's trying to get even with her over something that happened at their school when, in fact, Stevie's really been extra nice to her."

167

"And what was the Secret Santa thing that the other girl asked about?" said Eliot.

Lisa grimaced. She'd been so busy lately with everything else that she hadn't really given much thought to the Secret Santa gift, and now she was supposed to come up with something for Max by tomorrow night! "We drew names at our last Horse Wise meeting," she explained. "And we're supposed to do a good deed for the person whose name we drew. Tomorrow night at the party all the Secret Santas are supposed to be revealed."

"So who did you draw?" Eliot asked. "Not that Veronica creature, I hope."

"No, I drew Max, the owner of the stable. He's so busy you can hardly see him, much less figure out something nice to do for him for Christmas." Lisa sighed. "Now I've got to come up with something by tomorrow night."

"Gosh," said Douglas. "What to do for the man who does everything? That's a sticky wicket, all right."

Half a block away, a car turned down the street. Its shape looked familiar. Lisa peered at it under the streetlights. "Isn't that our car?"

"Looks like it," agreed Douglas. "Maybe they got worried and sent out a search party for us."

The car blinked its lights and pulled over to the side of the street. James Ross rolled down the window and stuck his head out into the cold night air.

"Hello, lads," he called. "Hi, Lisa. How did the singing go?"

"Great," Eliot said. "Did you come to give us a lift back?"

James grinned and shook his head. "Sorry. Richard's car has a flat battery at his office parking garage. I'm driving over to give him a spark. I should be done in a jiff." He smiled at Lisa. "Your mum says the clooty dumpling will be ready about the time we get back."

"Wonderful." Lisa tried to sound enthusiastic. They'd eaten Scottish food for the past ten meals, and she was beginning to dream about American hamburgers with ketchup-covered french fries and chocolate shakes.

"See you!" James waved and pulled back onto the street as the trio walked on home.

"So much for our lift," grumbled Eliot, pulling his cap down further over his ears.

"Oh, come on, El. It's brisk. Just like home." Douglas looked at his brother and gave an impish grin. "Beat you to the next post-box!"

With that both Eliot and Douglas began to run. They zigzagged crazily down the street, stopping first at one mailbox, then another. When they reached the end of the block they stopped, gasping for breath.

"You guys are nuts," Lisa said, laughing as she caught up with them.

"No, we're not," panted Eliot. "At home they'd call us mad."

"That may be," giggled Lisa. "But in America you're just plain nuts."

169

"Oh, come on," said Douglas. "Let's not stand here out in the cold arguing about how you call someone crazy. Let's get home. I'm getting very peckish!"

Lisa laughed as her cousins teased each other all the way up the driveway. Though sometimes it was a challenge to figure out exactly what they were saying, she liked them both a lot and she was glad they had come for Christmas.

"Just a few more steps." Douglas pretended to stagger with hunger as they walked through the empty garage to the kitchen door. "I can smell the clooty already."

"Actually I'm glad," admitted Lisa. "I'm getting hungry, too."

She opened the door. They all stepped into the kitchen together and stopped dead in their tracks. "Good grief!" Eliot cried. "What on earth has happened?"

Lisa's mouth fell open.

There, in her mother's formerly spotless kitchen, Caitlin and Fiona sat yowling in the middle of a mound of flour. The little girls were covered in the white stuff, with gobs of it in their hair and smeared all over their faces. Sarah Ross was crawling around on the floor on her hands and knees, fussing at the twins and desperately trying to clean everything up. Her face was bright red and she was frantically using a whiskbroom with one hand and a damp paper towel with the other. But the worst part was just in front of the oven. There sat Mrs. Atwood with huge runny pieces of clooty dumpling scattered all over the floor. The gooey stuff had splattered all over everything, and Mrs. Atwood's chin trembled, as if at any moment she might begin to cry. Lisa couldn't believe her eyes. In just a matter of moments, her mother's immaculate kitchen had become a complete disaster!

"Gosh." Douglas blinked in amazement. "Is this some sort of American Christmas custom?"

"Yes," said Lisa, suddenly bursting into a fit of giggles at the sight of four people covered in various amounts of flour. "It's called the Great American Pre-Christmas Flour Crawl."

Eliot began to laugh along with Lisa, and Douglas did, too. Mrs. Atwood looked up at them from her seat in front of the stove, and she, too, began to laugh. Sarah Ross, who'd been apologizing to Mrs. Atwood when she hadn't been scolding the twins, looked over and saw Mrs. Atwood laughing, and she began to laugh as well. Finally the twins, who'd been crying, stopped and looked at the adults around them. Nobody seemed angry at them anymore. In fact, everybody seemed to be covered in flour and suddenly having a marvelous time. They began to laugh along with everyone else.

Lisa felt a draft of chilly air as the back door opened behind her. She turned to see her father and James Ross coming through the door, their cheeks red from the cold. "You're not going to believe this, Dad," Lisa began, but she stopped when she saw both James and her father standing there, their eyes wide with amazement.

"Good heavens!" cried Mr. Atwood. "Is everyone all right? Did the stove blow up?"

"No, Richard, we're fine," gasped Mrs. Atwood, wiping tears of laughter from her eyes. She took one look at Sarah Ross, who had a piece of clooty dumpling dangling from her hair, and began to laugh all over again.

"I'm afraid it's our fault," giggled Sarah, trying to catch her breath. "The twins got into the flour and smeared it all over themselves and the kitchen. I came in here to clean it up, and then the clooty dumpling was ready. Eleanor had just taken it from the oven when she slipped on the flour and dropped the clooty and herself all over the floor!"

"At first I wanted to cry," laughed Mrs. Atwood. "Then I looked up and saw Lisa and Eliot and Douglas looking at us like we were crazy, and then I realized that we *were* crazy!" She started laughing all over again.

"It's certainly been the most memorable meal of our vacation," Sarah Ross said, collapsing on the floor in giggles. "The clooty dumpling that wasn't!"

James Ross and Mr. Atwood shook their heads at each other and smiled. "How about we help you guys clean up?" said Mr. Atwood as he rolled up the sleeves of his shirt. "Then why don't we just go out and get a hamburger for dinner?"

"Gosh, Dad, that would be wonderful," said Lisa. "I can't imagine anything that would taste quite as good right now."

They all pitched in and helped clean up the kitchen. James and Eliot and Mr. Atwood mopped up the floor while Sarah and Mrs. Atwood went to wash the clooty dumpling out of their hair. Douglas and Lisa were in charge of getting the twins free of flour. In a little while everyone reappeared in the kitchen, where all traces of the doomed dinner had disappeared.

"Okay," said Mr. Atwood as he put on his jacket. "Who's up for burgers and fries?"

"I am," cried Lisa.

"Me too," Douglas added with a grin.

"Then let's go."

They all piled into the Atwoods' station wagon and drove to a nearby restaurant that served the best hamburgers in Willow Creek. The hostess led them to a big table near a roaring fireplace, and everyone sat down to study the menu.

"I'll have the all-American cheeseburger and an order of french fries," James said when the waitress returned to take their order. "I've been dying to see how you chaps really eat in the States."

"Really?" said Mrs. Atwood. "I thought you'd want food that you were accustomed to. I thought it would make you feel more at home."

"Oh, don't misunderstand, Eleanor," said James. "Your meals have been fantastic, but sometimes it's fun to try new dishes."

"Yes," agreed Sarah, who held the squirming Fiona on

173

her lap. "It's all been delicious, but we're also keen to try some of your exotic American dishes."

"Goodness," said Mrs. Atwood with a laugh. "Then tomorrow night we'll order in pizza!"

Everyone ordered hamburgers along with James, and they all shared huge orders of french fries and onion rings. They had apple pie for dessert, then drove back home to the Atwoods' house.

"This is perfect timing," said Mr. Atwood as he took off his coat. "We're just in time to watch the game on TV. James, Douglas, Eliot, I'll pop some popcorn and we can settle back in the den for some serious football watching!"

"I'll join you later," said Eliot with a smile. "I need to practice a bit on my pipes."

Eliot went into the kitchen while Douglas and the two dads disappeared into the den. Lisa heard the football game begin to blare over the TV set just as various shrieks and wails from the bagpipes floated out of the kitchen. Caitlin and Fiona ran into the living room, covering their ears and singing some new song they'd heard on a children's TV show. Sarah Ross and Mrs. Atwood followed close behind, chatting about how groceries were so much more expensive in Scotland than America.

Lisa looked around. She could barely hear herself think. She didn't want to watch football or talk about Scottish groceries, and she certainly didn't want to go into the kitchen and listen to Eliot's squawking. Slowly

174

she turned and began to tiptoe upstairs to her room. Even though she was supposed to entertain Eliot and Douglas, there was so much going on down there that she was sure she wouldn't be missed.

She tiptoed into her bedroom and closed the door. She could still hear the din downstairs, but not quite as clearly as before. She smiled. Despite all the Scottish food and the disastrous clooty dumpling, the Rosses seemed to feel very much at home here, and she was glad. She lay down on her bed and closed her eyes. It felt good to be by herself for a moment, not to have to answer anybody's questions or show anybody where something was.

This must be what it's like for Max all the time, she thought suddenly. *When he's not dealing with us, he's teaching younger riders and older riders and worrying about the horses and tending to Maxi and telling Mrs. Reg and Red O'Malley what to do and ordering supplies on the telephone— and lately he's been even busier than usual.*

Suddenly she sat straight up in bed. She had just solved her Secret Santa problem. She knew exactly what she was going to do for Max. "I can't run the stable, but I can give him and Deborah a whole day and night of free baby-sitting," she said aloud. "They can go wherever they want and do whatever they want, all without having to worry about who's taking care of Maxi." She sighed as the wail of Eliot's bagpipes came drifting up from downstairs. "I can't imagine anything better than the gift of peace and quiet!"

LATE THE NEXT AFTERNOON the Horse Wise riders gathered in Pine Hollow's indoor riding ring. Phil and A.J. were there, and everyone was talking about the caroling and the Christmas party afterward.

"Where is Lisa?" Carole asked Stevie with a worried frown. "She's never late, and we should get going pretty soon if we're going to catch everyone around dinnertime."

"She'll be here." Stevie grinned. "Remember? You told me everyone has to be late sometime in their life."

"Yes, but not tonight! This is the most important night of the year!"

Suddenly a gasp went up from the carolers. Stevie and Carole looked toward the door. Lisa stood there in jeans

176

and a parka, and standing on either side of her were two magnificently dressed Scottish pipers!

"Lisa! Eliot! Douglas!" Stevie cried out, her eyes popping.

They walked into the ring. Eliot and Douglas wore red plaid kilts, bright red jackets, and black caps. Eliot carried his bagpipes over his left shoulder.

"Clan Ross reporting for duty, ma'am." Douglas grinned and gave Carole a snappy British salute.

Eliot patted his bagpipes affectionately. "We are armed and ready to sing!"

"Wow!" said Carol, amazed at the guys' wonderful outfits.

"Can you actually play that thing?" Stevie blinked at the gangly plaid bagpipes.

"Aye. Want to hear?" Eliot took a deep breath and put the chanter pipe in his mouth.

"Not here!" Lisa stopped him just as he was beginning to blow. "That really will put the horses off their feed!"

"You guys look terrific," said Carole. "You'll be the hit of Willow Creek!"

"Thanks." Douglas smiled. "Lisa told us about the Secret Santas, so we thought we'd surprise everyone and be Secret Scotsmen."

"Well, now that you're here, I guess we'd better get started." Carole stood up on a mounting block and tried to get everyone's attention. She had just opened her mouth to speak when another murmur of excitement went through the crowd. She looked again at the door, and once more couldn't believe her eyes. There stood the glamorous Tress Montgomery, and she was waving at Carole!

Carole hurried to the door, where Tress Montgomery was waiting for her, smiling. The same cameraman stood behind her, along with another man, who held a long microphone.

"Hi, Carole," Tress said warmly. "Remember me? I interviewed you and your dad the night of the burglary at the toy warehouse."

Carole could only nod. How could she possibly *not* remember Tress Montgomery and being on television?

"Good," Tress continued. "Deborah Hale called me yesterday and told me you guys had organized a carol singing to help the Marines. Would it be okay if we taped it? It's a terrific human interest story. They'll run it on the news tomorrow night." She looked around at the two kilted Scots mingling with the other singers and grinned. "This is such a great story, the national network might even pick it up."

"Sure," Carole said, her voice coming out in a nervous squeak. "That would be wonderful."

"Great. Then we'll go set up outside and wait for you guys to come out."

178

With that she disappeared down the hall, the two men trailing behind her. Carole felt as if she were walking through a dream, but she managed to hurry back to the mounting block.

"Okay, everybody," she announced, her voice sounding strong once again. "I've got some big news. Tress Montgomery's going to tape our caroling, and we're going to be on TV tomorrow night!"

An excited cheer went up from the carolers.

"But right now, we need to get going and raise some money for the Marines." Carole held up a nosebag Stevie handed her. "Stevie's borrowed Belle's own personal nosebag to keep our contributions in, so let's hit the streets and see if we can't come back with tons of money!"

"All right!" said Phil and A.J. together. Carole hopped off the mounting block, and she, Stevie, and Lisa began to lead the procession through the stable. The TV lights went on as soon as they emerged into the frosty night. They hadn't gone more than a few feet from Pine Hollow when Max's voice rang out behind them.

"Hey, Carole! Wait!"

Everyone stopped and looked back. Max stood in the entrance of the stable. He grinned and tugged once on a long lead rope. Prancer stepped out into the TV lights. She was wearing a bright red saddle blanket with brass sleigh bells sewn along the edges. White felt letters that read USMC CHRISTMAS TOY CAMPAIGN had been glued to both sides of the blanket. Prancer seemed to smile for the camera as the TV crew rushed in for a close-up.

"Wow!" breathed Carole along with everyone else. "Prancer looks magnificent!"

Max chuckled. "Well, I guess I'll have to tell you a little early, but I'm your Secret Santa. I thought helping you out with this campaign would be the special thing I could do for you." Max patted a saddlebag that was slung over Prancer's withers. "There's also a small contribution from Deborah and me inside here, to get you started on your way."

He grinned at the group as he handed Lisa Prancer's lead. "I hope all of you get so much money that Prancer will have to come home at a walk!" Just then Prancer nodded her head as if in agreement. Everyone laughed.

"Thanks, Max." Carole smiled at him. "Thanks so much!"

She looked at the group of carolers. Twenty kids, two Scotsmen, and a fabulously decorated horse. She knew already that this was going to be one night she'd remember for the rest of her life. It was almost too good to be true.

"Shall I pipe us out?" Eliot asked. "Surely I won't terrify any horses out here."

"Please do," said Carole. "Play something Christmassy!"

Eliot hurried to the front of the group, with the TV

crew close behind. He took several breaths to inflate his bagpipes, then turned and began to play. "O Come, All Ye Faithful" floated through the cold air as he marched slowly to the first house with all the carolers following him.

"Gosh," said Carole as she walked beside Prancer. "We've got a horse and a bagpiper and a TV news crew. Surely everyone in Willow Creek will give us money now."

"Well, we should certainly get everyone's attention!" Lisa said with a laugh.

At the first house, people were already waiting for them on the porch. "Mommy, look!" a little girl cried delightedly. "A horse with bells! And someone's playing that funny instrument!" The group sang "Jingle Bells," after which Carole ran up onto the porch and held the saddlebag out for a contribution.

"We've never seen anything like this before," the little girl's father said as he dropped a ten-dollar bill into the bag. "We're so glad you stopped by!"

"Thank you," Carole said. "And Merry Christmas!"

"Merry Christmas to all of you!" the man replied. He and his family stood waving as Eliot piped the carolers on to the next house.

Everyone loved the Pine Hollow singers. By the time they reached the last street they'd planned to carol on, one side of the saddlebag was almost full.

"Looks like we've got a lot of money," Lisa said as she

peered at the array of bills. "Don't you think we need to get back to Pine Hollow? Max said the Christmas party would start at eight sharp."

"Oh, let's carol on one more street," said Stevie. "This is so much fun, and if we take the shortcut through Mary Sanford's backyard, we can carol down Clayton Lane. That's the richest street in Willow Creek. Everybody who lives there is a millionaire!"

"Isn't there a creek at the bottom of the Sanfords' backyard?" Lisa asked worriedly.

"It's no big deal," Stevie answered. "We can all jump it."

"But you don't understand," Lisa said. "The last time I rode Prancer she was shying at all water crossings. She's gotten so she really hates them. She might even buck."

Carole shot a worried glance at Stevie. She thought she'd gotten Prancer over her fear of water, but what if she hadn't? If Prancer balked tonight, her whole Secret Santa project would be a flop. Still, she had to test her training method sometime, and there was a lot of money to be collected on Clayton Lane. She took a deep breath.

"Why don't we at least give it a try? Prancer might be so excited about running around at night with bells on that she'll forget her fear of water. Maybe if you get on one side of the creek and call her, she'll come across with me."

"Okay," Lisa agreed dubiously. "I guess it's worth a try." Eliot piped them down Mary Sanford's driveway. He jumped over the small creek, and the rest of the crowd followed. Soon only Stevie, Carole, Lisa, and Prancer were left on the other side.

"Come on, Lisa," Stevie said. "Let's jump over. If Prancer sees you on the other bank she might go over without any problems."

"Okay." Lisa and Stevie hopped over the creek while Carole led Prancer to the edge of the bank.

"Okay, girl," Carole whispered softly into Prancer's ear. "I know it's really cold tonight, but remember how easy this is, and how much fun it is to splash in the water."

"Come on, Prancer," Lisa called from the other side of the creek. "Come on over here, girl."

Prancer's ears pricked forward. Carole gave one gentle tug on her lead rope. Almost immediately the big horse stepped delicately across the creek, her sleigh bells jingling as she walked.

"I don't believe it!" Lisa cried. "It's a Christmas miracle! She's never been that calm around water!"

Carole began to giggle. "I hate to break the news, but it's no miracle. It's just a little retraining."

"Huh?" Lisa blinked.

Carole grinned. "I guess I may as well tell you now. I'm your Secret Santa. I knew Prancer's old fear of water had returned. My dad gave me this new book about horse training, so I tried one of the techniques out on Prancer. It worked!"

"So that's why Prancer was warm before our last couple of riding lessons!" Lisa said.

Carole nodded. "I've been working with her every day for the past week. We were Pine Hollow's best-kept secret!"

"Everybody knew?" Lisa asked.

"Well, Stevie, Max, and Mrs. Reg did," replied Carole. "And of course Prancer." She reached over and gave Lisa a hug. "Merry Christmas!"

"Thanks, Carole!" Lisa hugged Carole back. "Now I can ride in the competition next month!"

Eliot piped them down Clayton Lane, Tress Montgomery and the TV crew reporting all the way. At first everyone was a little nervous about walking up to the mansions that lined the street, but the residents came out to greet them just as warmly as the people on the other streets had done. Everyone loved Eliot's piping and Douglas's kilt and the way Prancer jingled with every step. "That horse reminds me of sleigh rides in Vermont," one man said as he dropped a twenty-dollar bill into the saddlebag.

They caroled down both sides of the street until they came to a dead end. There stood the grandest house on the street. It blazed with lights in every window, and all sorts of expensive black cars lined its driveway.

"Gosh," Lisa said. "It looks like they're having a party. Maybe we shouldn't disturb them."

"Oh, we may as well try," said Carole. "It's the last

house we've got to carol at, and they may give us some money."

"Yeah," agreed Stevie. "And when else are we going to get a chance to peek inside a house like that?"

"Well?" Eliot shifted the pipes on his shoulder. "Shall we give it a go?"

The girls looked at each other, then nodded. "Pipe on, Eliot!" said Carole.

"Stout lasses!" Eliot put the chanter back in his mouth and began to play. Slowly the group made its way up the hill, past all the parked cars. When everyone had gathered on the enormous front porch, Carole rang the doorbell, and Stevie led a rendition of "Silent Night." For what seemed like a long time, no one came to the door; then it swung open. Carole had just begun to say, "Toys for needy children campaign," when the words died in her mouth. Standing there, dressed in an elegant blue velvet gown, was the elderly woman who'd given them one of her two dollars in front of TD's!

"Good heavens!" The woman blinked at Carole and Stevie. "You're the girls who were collecting money at the mall!"

"And you were the poor lady who gave us your next-to-last dollar!" Stevie blurted out. Carole nudged Stevie quickly with her elbow, but the woman had heard what she'd said. She threw her head back and began to laugh.

"Well, I probably looked like that to you. I had just

come from my oil painting class, and I'd forgotten my purse. A classmate loaned me two dollars to get home. One of the dollars I gave to you, the other I used for bus fare." She laughed again. "No wonder you two thought I was a bag lady."

Stevie and Carole blushed with embarrassment, but the woman held the door open wide. She smiled at everybody—the carolers, Eliot, the TV crew, even Prancer in her fancy outfit.

"Please come in for some refreshments, all of you," she said. "Or at least all of you but the horse. We're having a party and we've plenty to spare!"

Lisa tied Prancer to a bush outside the house and joined the others inside. A party was indeed going on. Men dressed in tuxedos were chatting with women wearing elegant gowns. A woman was playing a grand piano in the huge living room while a black-coated butler served glasses of champagne from a huge silver tray.

The lady smiled at Carole. "If you'll let me pass this saddlebag around the living room, I expect you'll get some nice donations. Meanwhile, I'm going to see if I can find my purse so I can write you a check. I really admire you girls for being so determined to succeed. She turned to the butler. "Mason, would you see that our new guests get some refreshments?"

"Yes, Mrs. Llewellyn," the butler replied in a deep voice.

Mrs. Llewellyn took Carole's saddlebag into the living

room while Mason passed a huge tray of delicate Italian Christmas cookies among the carolers. By the time every caroler had taken a cookie, Mrs. Llewellyn had returned with the saddlebag bulging with money.

"Now, let me see," she said absentmindedly as she handed the saddlebag to Carole. "Where did I put that purse?"

"You might try the kitchen, madam," Mason intoned seriously. "I believe I last saw your handbag on top of the refrigerator."

"On top of the refrigerator?" Mrs. Llewellyn frowned. "What on earth is it doing there?" She shrugged and chuckled at Carole and Stevie. "Well, just a minute, girls. You never know where things are going to turn up in this house."

Mrs. Llewellyn hurried off down the hall. In a moment she returned with her battered purse in hand. "Well, Mason, you were right. Here it is."

She pulled a checkbook out of her purse and leaned over a small table to scribble out a check. She signed it with a flourish and stuffed it into the saddlebag with a smile. "There!" she said. "I thank you for stopping by my house, and I hope all of you have a wonderful holiday!" She grinned at everyone. "Would you sing another song before you leave?"

"Sure," said Stevie. She turned to Carole and smiled. "Let's sing your mother's Kwanzaa song."

"You think so?" Carole's eyes were bright.

187

Stevie turned to the carolers. "Okay, everybody. We're going to sing Carole's song. On three. One, two, three!"

All at once the song Carole's mother had taught her so long ago began to fill the huge house. The pianist stopped playing in the living room, and all the guests came to listen to the beautiful song about love, hard work, and sharing. When the carolers finished, the entire room burst into applause.

"Thank you so much," Mrs. Llewellyn finally said. "That was one of the loveliest songs I've ever heard."

"Thanks for everything," said Carole. "Merry Christmas!"

"Merry Christmas!" everyone called back.

Phil opened the huge front door, and with a chorus of "We Wish You a Merry Christmas," the carolers filed out into the chilly darkness. Lisa untied Prancer from the bush, and all the way back to Pine Hollow Eliot piped "Deck the Halls with Boughs of Holly."

"Gosh, Stevie, this is incredible. All those rich people in there must have given us a fortune!" whispered Carole as they sang their way back to the stable.

"I know," said Stevie, her eyes shining. "Everybody loved us and loved Eliot and Douglas and Prancer. I can hardly wait to get back and find out how much money we raised!"

20

By the time they returned to Pine Hollow, Christmas had come to the indoor riding ring. Evergreen garlands were fastened to the walls, dotted with colorful bunches of orange carrots and bright red apples. At one end of the ring stood a huge table covered with all sorts of Christmas treats, and at another table, Mrs. Reg smiled behind a bowl of hot apple cider. In the middle of the ring stood a Christmas tree decorated with a small treat for every horse in the stable and a small gift for every rider. Christmas music rang out from a stereo system Red O'Malley had set up. Maxi squealed with delight from Deborah's arms as Eliot and Prancer led the carolers back into the room.

"All right, all you Horse Wise Christmas carolers,"

Max announced as the group blinked at the wonderful decorations. "I hereby proclaim that this year's Christmas party has begun. You can now help yourselves to all these Christmas goodies and reveal your Secret Santas. Have a good time!"

Max grinned as everyone took off their jackets and headed toward the refreshment table. Then he turned to Lisa and Carole.

"How did the fund-raising go?" he asked excitedly.

"Wonderful!" replied Carole. "Everybody loved us, and everybody gave us lots of money!"

"Did Prancer do a good job?" Max asked, giving Prancer a rub between her ears.

"She was fabulous!" said Lisa. "She even walked through the creek in Mary Sanford's backyard!"

"Oh, so all that secret retraining worked, huh?" Max looked at Carole, his blue eyes twinkling.

"It sure did." Lisa grinned at Carole. "Now I can compete in the trail ride next month!"

"Well, since Prancer's had such a busy schedule lately, why don't you guys take her back to her stall and put her to bed? I'm sure she's exhausted from lugging around all that money." Max pulled the pretty red blanket off Prancer's back and handed the lead rope to Lisa.

"Come on, Prancer," said Lisa. "You've had a busy night."

"Can we come, too?" asked Douglas. "Eliot and I have never watched anyone put a horse to bed."

"Sure," giggled Lisa. "But Prancer's not nearly as hard to put to bed as Caitlin and Fiona are."

Carole watched as Lisa and her cousins led Prancer back to her stall. She turned to Stevie. "Why don't we go count our contributions and see how much money we made?"

"Good idea," said Stevie. "I bet we got at least fifty dollars at Mrs. Llewellyn's house."

"Why don't you use my office?" offered Max. "It's quiet in there, and you can spread everything out on my desk."

"Thanks, Max," said Carole. "That would be great."

Stevie and Carole grabbed a handful of cookies from the refreshment table and carried the heavy saddlebag to the office. Stevie turned on the lights, and Carole cleared some papers off Max's desk.

"Why don't you count one side of the bag and I'll count the other?" said Carole. "That way we won't get confused and we'll get done in half the time."

"Okay," Stevie agreed through a mouthful of chocolate chip cookie.

They sat down and began to count. Piles of five- and ten-dollar bills, along with a few checks, began to grow at both ends of the desk. Carole counted faster than Stevie, and in a few minutes she announced her total.

"Wow!" she cried. "I've got two hundred seventy-five dollars over here!"

"Wait a minute," said Stevie, frowning as she counted her last pile of tens. "I've got three hundred and ten. That makes five hundred and eighty-five altogether. That's great!"

"It sure is better than the nineteen dollars we got at the shopping center," Carole said. Then she gave a little sigh. "Of course, it'll never replace all those toys, but it'll help a little."

Stevie nodded. "Wait," she said, peering into her saddlebag. "There's something else in here." She reached in and pulled out a folded piece of blue paper. "Hey, here's a check I forgot to count."

She unfolded the check. Suddenly her eyes grew big as saucers. "Good golly!" she cried. She held the check out to Carole. "Am I reading this right?"

Carole examined the check closely. It was made out to the Marines and signed by Mrs. Llewellyn. On the amount line, the number one had been written, followed by four zeros. "Stevie!" Carole said barely above a whisper. "Mrs. Llewellyn just gave us ten thousand dollars!"

"That's what I thought it said," Stevie said in a trembly voice. "But you know how I am at math."

Carole blinked. "This is ten thousand dollars!" she cried, the figure finally sinking in. "Stevie, the lady we thought was a bag lady just gave us ten thousand dollars!" She looked at Stevie. "Now we can replace all the toys that were stolen!"

"This is the most incredible thing that's ever happened!" Stevie jumped up and threw her arms around

Carole. They hugged and danced a jig right in the middle of the office. "Let's go tell everybody," cried Carole. "They won't believe it!"

"Okay," Stevie agreed. "Let's go!"

They stuffed the check and the money back inside the saddlebag and ran to the indoor ring. The party was going strong. Tress Montgomery was wrapping up her news story, while the Horse Wise carolers were filling up on Christmas goodies and hot cider. Stevie and Carole raced to the center of the ring, just in front of the Christmas tree.

"Hey, everybody!" Stevie yelled. "Listen up! Carole has something to tell you!"

Everyone stopped talking and turned toward Carole. She threw the saddlebag over her shoulder and was just about to speak when she heard a loud *"Ten-hut"* at the door. She turned. Her father stood there at attention in his full dress uniform, with four other Marines lined up behind him. At a signal from him, they all marched forward. Carole felt the bright TV lights turn directly on her.

Her father stopped his troops in front of her and saluted, his brass buttons gleaming in the bright lights. "I understand that a contingent of Pine Hollow riders has tonight undertaken a mission of aid to the U.S. Marine Corps." Colonel Hanson smiled, but he spoke with great dignity.

"We have, sir," Carole said, saluting him smartly in

return. "The Pine Hollow riders are pleased to report that we are contributing a grand total of ten thousand, five hundred eighty-five dollars to the Christmas toy campaign!"

A gasp went up from the crowd. The TV cameraman zoomed in on Carole for a close-up.

"You're kidding!" Colonel Hanson said in amazement.

"No, Dad." Carole held up the saddlebag. "It's all right here! A lady we thought was poor turned out to be rich. She wrote us a check for ten thousand dollars!"

"Honey, that's fantastic!" Colonel Hanson stepped forward and gave Carole a big hug while the room erupted in cheers. The cameraman panned around the room, shooting the laughing and cheering carolers while Tress Montgomery spoke excitedly into the microphone in her hand.

Colonel Hanson turned to the four Marines and released them from attention. "Go enjoy the party for a few minutes, guys," he said with a smile. "I want to talk to these girls."

The Marines headed over to the refreshment table. Colonel Hanson smiled down at Stevie, Lisa, and Carole. "I just want to tell all three of you how proud I am of the Saddle Club," he said. "Ten thousand dollars is a wonderful gift, but even if you'd only raised ten dollars I'd have been just as pleased. You worked very hard and very unselfishly for people who are less fortunate than you. I couldn't be any prouder!"

194

He hugged them all, then gave Carole an extra-long hug and kissed the top of her head. "This is just the best Christmas ever, for me," he said, holding her close. "I wish we could stay longer, but we've got to get this money over to headquarters. We've got some toys to buy!" He kissed her again. "How about I pick you up later at Stevie's house?"

"That would be great, Dad," Carole said, holding her father close.

The Marines emptied all the money from the saddle-bag into a large sack and set off for the base. The party in the indoor ring continued, with the TV crew taping Eliot as he piped "Jingle Bells" to an admiring group of fans.

Lisa noticed that Max, Maxi, and Deborah were all standing by the punch bowl. Deborah had a cell phone to her ear, and Max was trying to juggle Maxi and a cup of cider. Lisa walked over to them.

"Hi," she said, taking Maxi, who held out her arms and went to Lisa happily. "Looks like you've got one too many things to handle."

"Thanks," Max replied with a tired smile. "Sometimes it gets pretty hard to take care of everything at once."

Lisa smiled back. As Deborah stashed her cell phone in her pocket, Lisa handed Max a small, handmade card.

"What's that?" Deborah asked. "A Christmas card?"

"Well, kind of," said Lisa. "Both of you read it to-gether."

Max unfolded the card and read aloud to Deborah. " 'This card entitles the bearer to one entire day and night of free baby-sitting, courtesy of your Secret Santa.' " He looked at Lisa and grinned.

"Is it you?"

Lisa nodded as Maxi planted a slurpy kiss on her cheek.

"Are you sure you want to volunteer for a whole day and night of Maxi?" Deborah asked.

"Oh, yes," said Lisa. "Max has been so nice to us all year, and if it hadn't been for you calling Tress Montgomery, Carole's toy drive wouldn't have been nearly the success that it was." Lisa gave a tired chuckle. "And anyway, after a few days of entertaining my six Scottish relatives, one little baby will seem like a vacation!"

"Gosh, Lisa, that's awfully nice," Max said. He winked at Deborah. "Shall we take her up on it tomorrow?"

Deborah laughed. "Let's give her a chance to catch her breath," she said. "We'll set up a time after the first of the year."

Lisa gave Maxi back to Deborah and went to join Douglas, who was giving Phil and A.J. lessons in the Scottish sword dance. Carole was passing a plateful of gingerbread around while Stevie talked to Eliot about his bagpipe.

"What do you call those big pipes that stick up over your shoulder?" Stevie asked, standing on tiptoe to touch the top one.

"Drones," replied Eliot. "They're all pitched to A."

196

"And you play the melody on this—" Before Stevie could finish her question, she felt a sharp tap on her shoulder. She turned around. Veronica diAngelo stood there, her green eyes blazing as never before.

"There you are, you little sneak!" she hissed. "You planned all this behind my back, didn't you?"

Stevie blinked. "Of course I planned it, Veronica. Along with Lisa and Carole. We called and told you about it. Only about thirty different people knew what was going on."

"Yes, but you left out one teeny tiny little detail, didn't you?" Veronica huffed.

"What was that?" Stevie asked, astonished.

"You just forgot to mention that small fact that a TV crew would be taping the whole thing. And I just heard Tress Montgomery tell her cameraman that the national network was going to show this on their special Christmas Eve broadcast! Everybody in America is going to be watching this!"

"Really?" Stevie's eyes lit up.

"Yes!" said Veronica. "You just forgot to mention that, didn't you?"

"I didn't know," replied Stevie. "None of us knew they were going to be here until they walked in the door. Deborah called them."

"Oh, sure, Stevie." Veronica rolled her eyes. "You knew I would be tied up doing that stupid play at school while all this was going on. You knew I was going to have to sing my solo in a dumb donkey costume, and you planned this just to get even!"

"No," said Stevie. "Really, Veronica, I didn't know!"

"Oh, please!" Veronica turned on her heel and stormed away.

"Well, Merry Christmas to you, too, Veronica!" Stevie called as the furious girl disappeared into the crowd. "By the way, I'm your Secret Santa! Hope you like how I cleaned all your tack!"

"Wow," said Eliot, who'd overheard the whole conversation. "She's really corked off at you!"

Stevie smiled. "Oh, well," she said with a shrug. "That's just Veronica. To know her is definitely *not* to love her!"

The party lasted for another hour. Then, in ones, twos, and threes, the carolers began to put on their coats and leave. Some were walking home, while others were being picked up by their parents.

"Let's say good-night to the horses before we go," said Stevie. "I feel like I haven't seen Belle in ages."

Lisa, Douglas, and Eliot walked down to bid Prancer another good-night while Stevie and Carole stopped by Belle's and Starlight's stalls. Both girls had pulled carrots off the wreaths in the indoor ring to give the horses. Belle was wide awake and ate hers in two gulps. Starlight, who'd been curled up asleep, gave Carole a soft whinny when he saw her and took the carrot gently from her hand.

"We're really lucky to have these guys," said Carole softly.

"We sure are," Stevie agreed. "We're lucky to have lots of things."

"Like horses and clothes and warm houses?" Carole asked.

"Yes," said Stevie. "But I was really thinking of friends." She looked over Carole's shoulder as Lisa and her cousins returned from Prancer's stall. "Friends both old and new."

Carole smiled. "You're absolutely right. We may not have ten thousand dollars like Mrs. Llewellyn, but we're just as rich as she is, friend-wise."

"Well," said Eliot as he came up and gave Starlight a pat on the nose. "Everyone ready to be piped home?"

"I think so," said Stevie. "I don't know about you guys, but I'm exhausted!"

Eliot and Douglas led them through the darkened stable. A few horses stirred in their sleep, but otherwise everything was silent. Just as they were about to step out into the cold night, Eliot and Douglas stopped.

"Oh, no," they said at once. "Hide your eyes! It's just too horrible to see!"

"What is it?" the girls cried, trying to see around Eliot and his cumbersome set of pipes. Stevie stepped around him and peered into the darkness.

"Oh, Carole!" she cried. "You got your wish!"

Carole and Lisa rushed out behind Stevie. It was true.

199

Carole had gotten her wish. Huge, lacy flakes of snow were falling thickly from the sky. The ground was already a powdery white, and the snow showed no sign of stopping.

"Oh, how wonderful!" Carole cried, looking up and letting the big wet flakes fall on her face. "This makes everything absolutely perfect!"

"No, I think something else makes this absolutely perfect," said Stevie.

"What?" Lisa asked.

"You guys do," Stevie said, smiling at Carole, Lisa, Douglas, and Eliot. "It's just what Carole said. We may not be rich in money, but we are very rich in friends!"

"You're absolutely right, Stevie," Lisa said as The Saddle Club and the two kilted boys locked arms and slowly began to walk home through the swiftly falling snow.

What happens to The Saddle Club next?
Read Bonnie Bryant's exciting new series
and find out.

High school. Driver's licenses. Boyfriends. Jobs.
    A lot of new things are happening, but one thing
remains the same: Stevie Lake, Lisa Atwood, and Carole Hanson are still best friends. However, even among
best friends some things do change, and problems can
strain any friendship . . . but these three can handle
it. Can't they?

Read an excerpt from Pine Hollow #1: *The Long Ride*.

PROLOGUE

"Do you think we'll get there in time?" Stevie Lake asked, looking around for some reassuring sign that the airport was near.

"Since that plane almost landed on us, I think it's safe to say that we're close," Carole Hanson said.

"Turn right here," said Callie Forester from the backseat.

"And then left up ahead," Carole advised, picking out directions from the signs that flashed past near the airport entrance. "I think Lisa's plane is leaving from that terminal there."

"Which one?"

"The one we just passed," Callie said.

"Oh," said Stevie. She gripped the steering wheel tightly and looked for a way to turn around without causing a major traffic tie-up.

"This would be easier if we were on horseback," said Carole.

"Everything's easier on horseback," Stevie agreed.

"Or if we had a police escort," said Callie.

"Have you done that?" Stevie asked, trying to maneuver the car across three lanes of traffic.

"I have," said Callie. "It's kind of fun, but dangerous. It makes you think you're almost as important as other people tell you you are."

Stevie rolled her window down and waved wildly at the confused drivers around her. Clearly, her waving confused them more, but it worked. All traffic stopped. She crossed the necessary three lanes and pulled onto the service road.

It took another ten minutes to get back to the right and then ten more to find a parking place. Five minutes into the terminal. And then all that was left was to find Lisa.

"Where do you think she is?" Carole asked.

"I know," said Stevie. "Follow me."

"That's what we've been doing all morning," Callie said dryly. "And look how far it's gotten us."

But she followed anyway.

ALEX LAKE REACHED across the table in the airport cafeteria and took Lisa Atwood's hand.

"It's going to be a long summer," he said.

Lisa nodded. Saying good-bye was one of her least favorite activities. She didn't want Alex to know how hard it was, though. That would just make it tougher on him. The two of them had known each other for four years—as long as Lisa had been best friends with Alex's twin sister, Stevie. But they'd only started dating six months earlier. Lisa could hardly believe that. It seemed as if she'd been in love with him forever.

"But it is just for the summer," she said. The words sounded dumb even as they came out of her mouth. The summer *was* long. She wouldn't come back to Virginia until right before school started.

"I wish your dad didn't live so far away, and I wish the summer weren't so long."

"It'll go fast," said Lisa.

"For you, maybe. You'll be in California, surfing or something. I'll just be here, mowing lawns."

"I've never surfed in my life—"

"Until now," said Alex. It was almost a challenge, and Lisa didn't like it.

"I don't want to fight with you," said Lisa.

"I don't want to fight with you, either," he said, relenting. "I'm sorry. It's just that I want things to be different. Not very different. Just a little different."

"Me too," said Lisa. She squeezed his hand. It was a way to keep from saying anything else, because she was afraid that if she tried to speak she might cry, and she hated it when she cried. It made her face red and puffy, but most of all, it told other people how she was feeling. She'd found it useful to keep her feelings to herself these days. Like Alex, she wanted things to be different, but she wanted them to be very different, not just a little. She sighed. That was slightly better than crying.

"I TOLD YOU SO," said Stevie to Callie and Carole.

Stevie had threaded her way through the airport terminal, straight to the cafeteria near the security checkpoint. And there, sitting next to the door, were her twin brother and her best friend.

"Surprise!" the three girls cried, crowding around the table.

"We just couldn't let you be the only one to say good-bye to Lisa," Carole said, sliding into the booth next to Alex.

"We had to be here, too. You understand that, don't you?" Stevie asked Lisa as she sat down next to her.

"And since I was in the car, they brought me along," said Callie, pulling up a chair from a nearby table.

"You guys!" said Lisa, her face lighting up with joy. "I'm so glad you're here. I was afraid I wasn't going to see you for months and months!"

She *was* glad they were there. It wouldn't have felt right if she'd had to leave without seeing them one more time. "I thought you had other things to do."

"We just told you that so we could surprise you. We did surprise you, didn't we?"

"You surprised me," Lisa said, beaming.

"Me too," Alex said dryly. "I'm surprised, too. I really thought I could go for an afternoon, just *one* afternoon of my life, without seeing my twin sister."

Stevie grinned. "Well, there's always tomorrow," she said. "And that's something to look forward to, right?"

"Right," he said, grinning back.

Since she was closest to the outside, Callie went and got sodas for herself, Stevie, and Carole. When she rejoined the group, they were talking about everything in the world except the fact that Lisa was going to be gone for the summer and how much they were all going to miss one another.

She passed the drinks around and sat quietly at the end of the table. There wasn't much for her to say. She didn't really feel as if she belonged there. She wasn't anybody's best friend. It wasn't as if they minded her being there, but she'd come along because Stevie had offered to drive her to a tack shop after they left the airport. She was simply along for the ride.

". . . And don't forget to say hello to Skye."

"Skye? Skye who?" asked Alex.

"Don't pay any attention to him," Lisa said. "He's just jealous."

"You mean because Skye is a movie star?"

"And say hi to your father and the new baby. It must be exciting that you'll meet your sister."

"Well, of course, you've already met her, but now she's crawling, right? It's a whole different thing."

An announcement over the PA system brought their chatter to a sudden halt.

"It's my flight," Lisa said slowly. "They're starting to board and I've got to get through security and then to Gate . . . whatever."

"Fourteen," Alex said. "It comes after Gate Twelve. There are no thirteens in airports."

"Let's go."

"Here, I'll carry that."

"And I'll get this one . . ."

As Callie watched, Lisa hugged Carole and Stevie. Then she kissed Alex. Then she hugged her friends again. Then she turned to Alex.

"I think it's time for us to go," Carole said tactfully.

"Write or call every day," Stevie said.

"It's a promise," said Lisa. "Thanks for coming to the airport. You, too, Callie."

Callie smiled and gave Lisa a quick hug before all the girls backed off from Lisa and Alex.

Lisa waved. Her friends waved and turned to leave her alone with Alex. They were all going to miss her, but the girls had one another. Alex only had his lawns to mow. He needed the last minutes with Lisa.

"See you at home!" Stevie called over her shoulder, but she didn't think Alex heard. His attention was completely focused on one person.

Carole wiped a tear from her eye once they'd rounded a corner. "I'm going to miss her."

"Me too," said Stevie.

Carole turned to Callie. "It must be hard for you to understand," she said.

"Not really," said Callie. "I can tell you three are really close."

"We are," Carole said. "Best friends for a long time. We're practically inseparable." Even to her the words sounded exclusive and uninviting. If Callie noticed, she didn't say anything.

The three girls walked out of the terminal and found their way to Stevie's car. As she turned on the engine, Stevie was aware of an uncomfortable empty feeling. She really didn't like the idea of Lisa's being gone for the summer, and her own unhappiness was not going to be helped by a brother who was going to spend the entire time moping about his missing girlfriend. There had to be something that would make her feel better.

"Say, Carole, do you want to come along with us to the tack shop?" she asked.

"No, I can't," Carole said. "I promised I'd bring in the horses from the paddock before dark, so you can just drop me off at Pine Hollow. Anyway, aren't you due at work in an hour?"

Stevie glanced at her watch. Carole was right. Everything was taking longer than it was supposed to this afternoon.

"Don't worry," Callie said quickly. "We can go to the tack shop another time."

"You don't mind?" Stevie asked.

"No. I don't. Really," said Callie. "I don't want you to be late for work—either of you. If my parents decide to get a pizza for dinner again, I'm going to want it to arrive on time!"

Stevie laughed, but not because she thought anything was very funny. She wasn't about to forget the last time she'd delivered a pizza to Callie's family. In fact, she wished it hadn't happened, but it had. Now she had to find a way to face up to it.

As she pulled out of the airport parking lot, a plane roared overhead, rising into the brooding sky. *Maybe that's Lisa's plane*, she thought. The noise of its flight seemed to mark the beginning of a long summer.

The first splats of rain hit the windshield as Stevie paid their way out of the parking lot. By the time they were on the highway, it was raining hard. The sky had darkened to a steely gray. Streaks of lightning brightened it, only to be followed by thunder that made the girls jump.

The storm had come out of nowhere. Stevie flicked on the windshield wipers and hoped it would go right back to nowhere.

The sky turned almost black as the storm strengthened. Curtains of rain ripped across the windshield, pounding on the hood and roof of the car. The wipers flicked uselessly at the torrent.

"I hope Fez is okay," said Callie. "He hates thunder, you know."

"I'm not surprised," said Carole, trying to control her voice. It seemed to her that there were a lot of things Fez hated. He was as temperamental as any horse she had ever ridden.

Fez was one of the horses in the paddock. Carole didn't want to upset Callie by telling her that. If she told Callie he'd been turned out, Callie would wonder why he hadn't just been exercised. If she told Callie she'd exercised him, Callie might wonder if he was being overworked. Carole shook her head. What was it about this girl that made Carole so certain that whatever she said, it would be wrong? Why couldn't she say the one thing she really needed to say?

Still, Carole worked at Pine Hollow, and that meant taking care of the horses that were boarding there—and that meant keeping the owners happy.

"I'm sure Fez will be fine. Ben and Max will look after him," Carole said.

"I guess you're right," said Callie. "I know he can be difficult. Of course, you've ridden him, so you know that, too. I mean, that's obvious. But it's spirit, you see. Spirit is the key to an endurance specialist. He's got it, and I think he's got the makings of a champion. We'll work together this summer, and come fall . . . well, you'll see."

Spirit—yes, it was important in a horse. Carole knew that. She just wished she understood why it was that Fez's spirit was so irritating to her. She'd always thought of herself as someone who'd never met a horse she didn't like. Maybe it was the horse's owner . . .

"Uh-oh," said Stevie, putting her foot gently on the brake. "I think I got it going a little too fast there."

"You've got to watch out for that," Callie said. "My father says the police practically lie in wait for teenage drivers. They love to give us tickets. Well, they certainly had fun with me."

"You got a ticket?" Stevie asked.

"No, I just got a warning, but it was almost worse than a ticket. I was going four miles over the speed limit in our hometown. The policeman stopped me, and when he saw who I was, he just gave me a warning. Dad was furious—at me and at the officer, though he didn't say anything to the officer. He was angry at him because he thought someone would find out and say I'd gotten special treatment! I was only going four miles over the speed limit. Really. Even the officer said that. Well, it would have been easier if I'd gotten a ticket. Instead, I got grounded. Dad won't let me drive for three months. Of course, that's nothing compared to what happened to Scott last year."

"What happened to Scott?" Carole asked, suddenly curious about the driving challenges of the Forester children.

"Well, it's kind of a long story," said Callie. "But—"

"Wow! Look at that!" Stevie interrupted. There was an amazing streak of lightning over the road ahead. The dark afternoon brightened for a minute. Thunder followed instantly.

"Maybe we should pull off the road or something?" Carole suggested.

"I don't think so," said Stevie. She squinted through the windshield. "It's not going to last long. It never does when it rains this hard. We get off at the next exit anyway."

She slowed down some more and turned the wipers up a notch. She followed the car in front of her, keeping a constant eye on the two red spots of the car's taillights. She'd be okay as long as she could see them. The rain pelted the car so loudly that it was hard to talk. Stevie drove on cautiously.

Then, as suddenly as it had started, the rain stopped. Stevie spotted the sign for their exit, signaled, and pulled off to the right and up the ramp. She took a left onto the overpass and followed the road toward Willow Creek.

The sky was as dark as it had been, and there were clues that there had been some rain there, but nothing nearly as hard as the rain they'd left on the interstate. Stevie sighed with relief and switched the windshield wipers to a slower rate.

"I think I'll drop you off at Pine Hollow first," she said, turning onto the road that bordered the stable's property.

Pine Hollow's white fences followed the contour of the road, breaking the open, grassy hillside into a sequence of paddocks and fields. A few horses stood in the fields, swishing their tails. One bucked playfully and ran up a hill, shaking his head to free his mane in the wind. Stevie smiled. Horses always seemed to her the most welcoming sight in the world.

"Then I'll take Callie home," Stevie continued, "and after that I'll go over to Pizza Manor. I may be a few minutes late for work, but who orders pizza at five o'clock in the afternoon anyway?"

"Now, now," teased Carole. "Is that any way for you to mind your Pizza Manors?"

"Well, at least I have my hat with me," said Stevie. Or did she? She looked into the rearview mirror to see if she could spot it, and when that didn't do any good, she glanced over her shoulder. Callie picked it up and started to hand it to her.

"Here," she said. "We wouldn't want— Wow! I guess the storm isn't over yet!"

The sky had suddenly filled with a brilliant streak of lightning, jagged and pulsating, accompanied by an explosion of thunder.

It startled Stevie. She shrieked and turned her face back to the road. The light was so sudden and so bright that it blinded her for a second. The car swerved. Stevie braked. She clutched at the steering wheel and then realized she couldn't see because the rain was pelting even harder than before. She reached for the wiper control, switching it to its fastest speed.

There was something to her right! She saw something move, but she didn't know what it was.

"Stevie!" Carole cried.

"Look out!" Callie screamed from the backseat.

Stevie swerved to the left on the narrow road, hoping it would be enough. Her answer was a sickening jolt as the car slammed into something solid. The car spun around, smashing against the thing again. When the thing screamed, Stevie knew it was a horse. Then it disappeared from her field of vision. Once again, the car spun. It smashed against the guardrail on the left side of the road and tumbled up and over it as if the rail had never been there.

Down they went, rolling, spinning. Stevie could hear the screams of her friends. She could hear her own voice, echoing in the close confines of the car, answered by the thumps of the car rolling down the hillside into a gully. Suddenly the thumping stopped. The screams were stilled. The engine cut off. The wheels stopped spinning. And all Stevie could hear was the idle *slap, slap, slap* of her windshield wipers.

"Carole?" she whispered. "Are you okay?"

"I think so. What about you?" Carole answered.

"Me too. Callie? Are you okay?" Stevie asked.

There was no answer.

"Callie?" Carole echoed.

The only response was the girl's shallow breathing.

How could this have happened?

ABOUT THE AUTHOR

Bonnie Bryant is the author of nearly a hundred books about horses, including The Saddle Club series, Saddle Club Super Editions, and the Pony Tails series. She has also written novels and movie novelizations under her married name, B. B. Hiller.

Ms. Bryant began writing The Saddle Club in 1986. Although she had done some riding before that, she intensified her studies then and found herself learning right along with her characters Stevie, Carole, and Lisa. She claims that they are all much better riders than she is.

Ms. Bryant was born and raised in New York City. She still lives there, in Greenwich Village, with her two sons.

Don't miss the next
exciting Saddle Club adventure . . .

HORSE FEVER
Saddle Club #85

January is the cruelest month, at least for The Saddle Club. The weather is miserable: cold and rainy. No one can go riding outside, and everyone is sick and tired of staying inside. The only things left to do are clean tack and ride around the indoor ring. The Saddle Club is bored—bored with riding and even with horses. So what can they do? Stevie thinks a little time in the kitchen whipping up treats sounds like a great idea, until a crazy bet with her brother gets her in big trouble. Now it's up to Lisa to help Stevie get out of the kitchen and back into shape. Meanwhile, Carole gets the opportunity to ride a championship horse, and suddenly she's thinking about selling Starlight. Will the friends rediscover their love for their horses? Or is The Saddle Club about to untack for good?